FAIR WARNING

"Don't do anything stupid," Fargo warned the two men.

One spun, drew a knife from inside his shirt, and threw it, all in one quick motion. Fargo fired off a shot but saw it go wide as the knife grazed his arm. Both men dived for their guns. The bearded one got to his first. Fargo's big Henry sounded, and the man, in a half crouch, never got his gun up as he fell to the ground in a stain of red.

Fargo dived sideways as the wide-faced man reached his gun and came up firing. Rolling across the ground, Fargo fired the big Henry with a low trajectory of shots.

"Ow, Jesus," the man cried and sprawled on the ground, clutching his calf.

"Drop it," Fargo ordered, but the man brought the revolver up again.

Fargo fired two shots, and the figure bucked upward before collapsing to twitch for a moment and then go rigid.

Some men were just born dumb, the Trailsman thought, and they died the same way. . . .

**BE SURE TO READ THE
OTHER BOOKS IN THIS EXCITING
TRAILSMAN SERIES!**

FALCONER'S LAW
BY JASON MANNING

The year is 1837. The fur harvest that bred a generation of dauntless, daring mountain men is growing smaller. The only way for them to survive is the way westward, across the cruelest desert in the West, over the savage mountains, through hostile Indian territory, to a California of wealth, women, wine, and ruthless Mexican authorities.

Only one man can meet that brutal challenge—His name is Hugh Falconer—and his law is that of survival....

from **SIGNET**

Prices slightly higher in Canada.   (0-451-18645-1—$5.50)

THE TRAILSMAN
#171

DEAD MAN'S RIVER

by

Jon Sharpe

A SIGNET BOOK

SHARPE

SIGNET
Published by the Penguin Group
Penguin Books USA Inc., 375 Hudson Street,
New York, New York 10014, U.S.A.
Penguin Books Ltd, 27 Wrights Lane,
London W8 5TZ, England
Penguin Books Australia Ltd, Ringwood,
Victoria, Australia
Penguin Books Canada Ltd, 10 Alcorn Avenue,
Toronto, Ontario, Canada M4V 3B2
Penguin Books (N.Z.) Ltd, 182–190 Wairau Road,
Auckland 10, New Zealand

Penguin Books Ltd, Registered Offices:
Harmondsworth, Middlesex, England

First published by Signet, an imprint of Dutton Signet,
a division of Penguin Books USA Inc.

First Printing, March, 1996
10 9 8 7 6 5 4 3 2 1

The Trailsman

Beginnings . . . they bend the tree and they mark the man. Skye Fargo was born when he was eighteen. Terror was his midwife, vengeance his first cry. Killing spawned Skye Fargo, ruthless, cold-blooded murder. Out of the acrid smoke of gunpowder still hanging in the air, he rose, cried out a promise never forgotten.

The Trailsman they began to call him all across the West: searcher, scout, hunter, the man who could see where others only looked, his skills for hire but not his soul, the man who lived each day to the fullest, yet trailed each tomorrow. Skye Fargo, the Trailsman, and the seeker who could take the wildness of a land and the wanting of a woman and make them his own.

1860 . . . the river.

DeSoto knew the river, Marquette and Jolliet sailed its vast reaches, as did the Sioux, the Iowa, the Osage, Choctaw, Natchez, and the Canadian fur trappers. It was the link that tied together the new land—from the north to the south, from pine forests to cotton fields, from the frigid lakes of Minnesota to the warmth of the Gulf of Mexico—a watery avenue for glittering riverboats and humble keelboat barges.

It was properly named the Mississippi, but it had many names. The Indians called it the Father of Waters, to some it was the Big Muddy, and to others it was a place that could swallow up bodies as easily as bales . . . the dead man's river.

1

He swore at himself when he thought about why he'd agreed to take part in it. It wasn't like him to respond to a dare, to sneers and taunts. But he had and now he realized why. Not for himself, but for a friend—a special friend. He'd done it for the Ovaro. He'd refused to let them run down a faithful companion who'd saved his life time and again. He'd refused to let them look with disdain on a friend they couldn't match. They were shallow men who believed only in what money could buy. A horse, like their women and fine houses, was but another possession. They understood owning, not caring, mastery, not loyalty.

But this was Missouri, a state half-free and half-slave, where cruelty was accepted and excess was almost a virtue. The eight men wore their wealth with disdainful arrogance. All were prominent horse farm owners who had gathered for their annual competition. Fargo was there only because Bob Fletcher had invited him to watch the event after he'd delivered a small herd of Brahmin steers to the Fletcher ranch. One of the owners, a tall, thin-faced man named Reilly, with a mouth that wore a perpetual sneer, had been the first to appraise the Ovaro as Fargo dismounted. "You here to enter the meet, mister?" he'd asked.

"No," Fargo said and Bob Fletcher cut in.

"Fargo's here as my guest," he explained.

"That's smart," the man said, his eyes on the magnificent Ovaro with the jet-black fore and hind quarters and pure white midsection. "Flashy horse but no real class," he added.

"Too much peasant blood in him," a short man who Bob Fletcher introduced as Hal Dorrance said. "All looks but no real substance. Sorry to be so harsh," the man added smugly.

Fargo's smile was tight. "Sorry you're such a bad judge of horseflesh," he said evenly.

A ripple of derisive laughter went through the others. One, a man named Frank Browder, dressed in the finest of riding clothes, custom-made jodhpurs, and a silk shirt, added words to his laughter. "Just look at our horses, old man. You don't really think your horse could stand up to any of them, do you?" he said. Fargo let his eyes move across the horses the others had brought to the meet. He took in beautifully groomed mounts, mostly standardbreds, Morgans, hackneys, a few Arabians and tightly-bred quarterhorses. He went over each of the horses, decided they were all good specimens but that none were outstanding. His smile stayed tight as he returned his gaze to the men.

"I'll take my Ovaro," Fargo said.

"That must be pure sentiment," one of the others said.

"Softheartedness precedes softheadedness," Frank Browder put in, his tone infuriating.

"I think your friend Fargo could use a lesson," Dorrance said to Bob Fletcher.

"Such as?" Fargo asked.

"Put your horse in the meet," Dorrance said. "Each of us enters one horse. It'll show you the difference between looks and substance. It'll show you what good breeding means."

Fargo felt anger rising inside himself. They had no right to run down the Ovaro. They were a smug, arrogant set of bastards. Bob Fletcher's voice broke into his thoughts. "My good friends have a lot of cruelty in them. You don't have to lend yourself to their little games, Fargo," he said.

But Dorrance wasn't to be dissuaded. "The winner gets one hundred dollars from each of the losers, just to make it sporting. You could learn about quality horses, Fargo."

Fargo let his lips purse. He wouldn't play their games for their pleasure. He'd get more out of them, something worthwhile. He thought about Charlie Lewis with his place in south Missouri. For the last twenty years Charlie had kept a place for old and worn horses, faithful companions who'd given their masters a lifetime of service and loyalty until age took its toll. Charlie Lewis figured they deserved to spend their last years in relaxation and happiness and he provided them a place for that. But he was always hard-pressed for money to keep up his place. Fargo brought his eyes to where the others waited.

"You all know Charlie Lewis, I'd guess," he said.

"Everybody knows about old Charlie and his home," Dorrance said, faint disdain in his voice. Fargo's eyes hardened but he kept his smile in place.

"You gents send any prize money I win to Charlie Lewis," Fargo said.

"My, you are an optimist," Frank Browder said. "But we've no problem with the stipulation."

"Then it's settled. You'll compete, Fargo," Hal

11

Dorrance said, turning and gesturing to the land behind where they stood. "We've a race with jumps for the field horses and good flat stretches for the thoroughbreds. After the race we've a test of jumps set up with moveable bars for height competition. Lastly we've those barrels over there to test a horse's strength and skill at tight cornering. That's to show how well our mounts can do polo or steer roping work."

"Maybe you'd like to walk the course first," Bob Fletcher said to Fargo.

"No need. I've been looking at it," Fargo said, his eyes scanning the far ends of the course marked out with ribboned poles. He kept a grim smile inside himself. The flat stretches they'd laid out were not really racetrack flat. The ground was rough and uneven. Their jumps were stone and pole with three-hedge and open-ditch hurdles. He grunted to himself. They were too smug to realize they'd made a mistake by urging him to compete. None of their horses would do their best on a course with so many rough edges. They had been too nicely bred, even the quarter horse stock. Against each other, their problems would be leveled out, but they weren't going to race just against each other, Fargo noted in silent satisfaction.

He stroked the Ovaro's powerful trapezius muscle and spoke softly as he climbed into the saddle. "You heard the things they said about you, old friend. You picked up on their attitude. It's time for us to do some teaching."

He turned the Ovaro to where the others were lining up to start the race. Most of the horses were brown or bay but Reilly rode a tall gray mount. He saw that Frank Browder and Hal Dorrance were on foot to one side, their horses mounted by two substitute riders, both hardly past their teens. They were undoubtedly their most talented exercise boys, chosen because they were light, young, and strong. But like their horses they were very short on experience. He was certain they'd be easily flustered, and he smiled again, bringing the Ovaro to the right end of the line.

Bob Fletcher brought out a small pistol and held it up into the air. "Ready, gentlemen . . . I'll fire on three. One . . . two . . . three!" he said and the sound of the gun going off all but drowned his last word. Browder's reddish-brown mount got off first, his rider sending him all-out at once. Reilly's gray was at his heels, then Hal Dorrance's horse and the others bunching up close behind. Fargo sent the Ovaro on the heels of the last two horses. He kept the Ovaro moving easily and closed the distance as the others slowed for the first jump, a fieldstone wall. He watched Browder's mount take the jump. The horse took it easily enough but his young rider had him going too fast and Fargo saw the horse have trouble holding his stride as he landed. The others jumped on his heels, most too eager, also, losing power and coordination on their jumps.

Fargo kept the Ovaro on their heels, the pinto moving with almost effortless ease. Browder opened up his lead on the next flat stretch, only to have it narrowed as two pole and stone jumps came up in quick succession. The field spread out as they took the jumps and Reilly's long-legged gray took the lead at the second jump. Fargo kept the Ovaro at the same pace and gained a few feet to put him in line with the last two horses. The next stretch was terrain that was fashioned of deep ridges and Reilly's gray immediately slowed and refused to go faster at its rider's whip. Dorrance's horse did the same, as Frank Browder's horse and the others fell back further. The Ovaro never slackened its easy pace and was suddenly behind the three lead horses. Fargo saw the two young riders glance back at him in surprise and Reilly throw a frown his way.

A stone jump came next, perhaps the highest of the lot. Reilly led the way across it by a half-length but again took the jump too fast and the gray had trouble keeping its footing as it touched down on the other side of the stone wall. Fargo held the Ovaro back in order to stay just behind the other three horses and he squinted ahead to see two more jumps, a hedge-covered stone fence and a post and rail fence. Fargo held the Ovaro close and as the horses neared the first of the two jumps he saw the two young riders bring their mounts closer together to keep him blocked behind.

Fargo leaned forward and let a series of Cheyenne war whoops roll from his lips. In an automatic reaction, the Ovaro tightened its muscles and surged forward, plunging in between the two horses in front of it. Fargo saw the glances of surprise and alarm from the two young riders and their horses instantly swerved away. They tried to rein their mounts back in but all this did was break their movement. Dorrance's horse hit the stone fence as it took the jump sideways and went down with its rider. Browder's horse managed to clear the jump but went down on the other side as it landed off balance. The Ovaro sailed over the jump with perfect balance to land alongside Reilly on the tall gray and he saw Reilly's perpetual sneer had changed to tight-lipped alarm. The gray veered outwards as Fargo let the Ovaro almost brush up against him.

"No, goddammit," Reilly swore as he yanked at his horse to straighten him out. But the gray balked, fought the rein and it took Reilly a half-dozen seconds to bring his horse back under control. Fargo and the Ovaro were at the last jump by then and took the post and rail hurdle with unbroken stride. On the other side, Fargo glanced back to see Reilly had cleared the jump, the two young riders close behind, but now the Ovaro was racing full-out, driving with all the strength of his powerful hindquarters. The stretch to the finish line was uneven land, replete with bumps and Fargo saw the three horses behind him shorten their strides. He let a smile touch his lips as he crossed the finish line only a few dozen yards from where the race had started. He eased the pinto to a canter, then a trot and came to a halt in front of Bob Fletcher, Hal Dorrance, and Frank Browder.

Bob grinned as stone-faced Dorrance and Fletcher watched their two young riders ride up. "Get off. I'll take him for the jumps," Dorrance growled at the boy.

"Same here," Frank Browder muttered as Reilly came to a halt alongside Fargo.

"None of our horses performed well," the man said. "You were lucky."

"We'll see," Fargo said.

"You've fifteen minutes to rest your horse before the jumps," Browder said and strode away. Fargo led the Ovaro under a wide-branched honey locust and rummaged in his saddlebag to bring out a small vial of ointment—a mixture of wintergreen, agrimony, and burdock root. He rubbed the ointment thoroughly into the horse's legs. It was a quick-acting, soothing relief for the muscle strain that would take effect immediately. The Ovaro was made of muscle power but he was not bred for jumping and Fargo knew he'd need as much help as he could get. He massaged the horse's legs vigorously and was finished when the fifteen minutes came to an end. The jump was in place, he saw, as he chose to be last.

He swung into the saddle and eyed the marks alongside the top pole. They measured five feet even and Fargo watched Hal Dorrance jump first on his reddish-brown horse. Reilly on his long-legged gray followed and then came the others. The Ovaro took the jump effortlessly. It was a clean jump for everyone. The top pole was raised five inches and they went into the second jump. Two of the horses dislodged the top pole and were eliminated. The top bar was raised another three inches to make the jump five feet eight inches. Three more of the horses knocked off the top pole leaving Dorrance, Frank Browder, Reilly, and Fargo. The bar was raised again, this time to six feet, a formidable height.

Dorrance went first, brought his horse back to give it a longer run. But Dorrance wasn't used to a long run and Fargo saw him fail to collect his horse on the approach. He took the jump too soon, his mount uncontained, and knocked off the two top poles as he went down to land. Browder was next and he took a long run, also, but he tried to hurry his horse by racing down to the jump and when his mount lifted to jump he was uncollected, most of the spring in his legs left behind. He slammed into the top pole and sent it down with an especially hard clatter. Reilly was next. He decided against a long run and sent his gray toward the jump at a held-in canter. It would have worked well enough on a lower jump but the gray, using his instinctive horse sense, realized he wasn't ready for the jump and balked. Reilly went flying over his neck to crash into the barrier where the others helped him regain his feet.

"Refusal. Disqualified," Fletcher called out and Fargo brought the Ovaro to the approach. He paused, let the horse eye the height, back up a few paces, and then move forward in prancing steps. He knew the Ovaro, knew the horse was gathering itself, very aware the jump was at the top of its range.

"Let's go, friend," Fargo whispered and flicked the reins against the jet-black neck. He let the Ovaro go at the jump on his own, keeping his own body moving with the horse's motion, his contact with his mount even and his weight well forward as the Ovaro leaped. Fargo murmured encouragement and the Ovaro sailed over the jump, stretched out for all the air space he could manage. But Fargo felt his rear hooves hit the top pole, forced himself to wait till the horse's forefeet touched ground before turning in the saddle to look back. The top bar shuddered, teetered on its cradle, rolled forward, hung for a split second and then rolled back and stayed in place.

Fargo let a sigh of relief escape and heard a muttered grumble go up from the others, partly chagrin and partly reluctant admiration. He slowed the Ovaro to a walk, guided the horse in a wide circle as the heavy barrels were set in place. Bob Fletcher strode forward, a pocket watch in his hand. "A horse that knocks over a barrel is disqualified," he said. "Time decides the winner." He stepped back, starter's pistol in hand as Dorrance brought his horse to the starting line. Fargo's glance took in the dozen barrels that had been placed in a tight, zigzag pattern. He moved the Ovaro slowly, confidently. The last challenge was made for the pinto. A fast time would depend on the ability to corner tight and swerve fast and that took compact, powerful hindquarters. Another quick glance at the other horses told him that none had the muscled rump to match the Ovaro's and he drew to a halt as Dorrance came to the starting line. Fletcher motioned him to start and Dorrance sent his horse out fast. He did fairly well until he started to work his way back through the barrels and Fargo saw the horse lose power.

He failed to cut tightly on the last six barrels and ended with a time of two minutes ten seconds. Another starter took his place, followed by two more and all were from five to ten seconds slower than Dorrance. Reilly moved into place with his long-legged gray and Fargo almost predicted his poor showing. He moved the Ovaro forward as Frank Browder started his run. The man had the horse with the best hindquarters of the lot and when he finished the run he held the lead with a time of one minute and fifty-five seconds.

But the smugness in his face turned into a glower at Fargo's smile. Fargo walked the Ovaro to the starting line, nodded to Fletcher who brought his arm down in a chopping motion. Fargo kicked his heels against the Ovaro's ribs, kept a tight rein and sent the horse swerving around the first barrel. At a touch of the reins, the pinto used his massive hindquarter muscles to swing around and streak for the next barrel. He cornered again, hardly slowing, swerved around the obstacle and went onto the next and the next and when he surged forward around the last barrel, Bob Fletcher's voice rang out. "One minute and thirty-three seconds," he said as Fargo brought the Ovaro to a halt and patted the horse's glistening black neck.

Frank Browder approached first, Reilly and

Dorrance at his heels. They were gentlemen enough to swallow their disappointment with good manners if not quite graciousness. "Quite an exhibition, Fargo," Dorrance said.

"Guess there's something to be said for peasant blood," Fargo remarked.

Browder managed a wry half-smile. "Perhaps, or perhaps we haven't done as good a job of breeding as we thought."

"As I figure it, you'll be sending two thousand four hundred dollars to Charlie Lewis—a hundred dollars from each of you for each event," Fargo said.

"Yes, an amount considerably larger than we usually divide amongst ourselves," Dorrance said.

"But you'll be sending it," Fargo said, his voice hardening.

"That sounds a little threatening, my friend," the man said.

"Let's just say you won't be happy if I have to come back collecting it," Fargo said with a thin smile.

"It'll be sent. You have our word as Missouri gentlemen," Dorrance said.

"Good," Fargo said, reining in the first reply that came to his lips. "That'll keep a lot of Charlie Lewis's old friends eating for a long time." He backed the Ovaro and offered a nod that took in everyone. "It's been a pleasure," he said as he put the pinto into a trot and received a wave and a wide smile from Bob Fletcher. He rode north, kept the horse at a slow trot and moved into the richness of the Missouri countryside. He rode leisurely, enjoyed the good green foliage and rolling hills. He had time to spare, his next job not scheduled for another month up in Dakota territory. When he crossed over the tops of low hills he could see the blue ribbon that was the Mississippi to his right as it curved and twisted its way along. At one spot, when a ridge he rode turned east, he caught sight of two majestic paddlewheelers and a good deal of cultivated plantation land bordering the river.

But as he went on, the land turned wild again, traversed only by a few roads and open land mixed in with heavy growths of horse chestnut, red ash, hackberry and cottonwoods. It was nearly dusk when he became aware of the movement at his rear, a good distance behind yet, and he paused on a rise to peer at the foliage. No idle breeze, he noted. Horses and riders, making their way in a group. At least four, maybe six, he estimated. With the experience of a top tracker, Fargo followed their movements by studying the motion of the leaves, the dip of the branches that were pushed aside and snapped back. They rode carefully, he saw, slowing often, then going on. They were searching for a trail as well as scanning the terrain.

The dusk deepened and Fargo turned north again, found a hollow in a cluster of hackberry as night descended and bedded down. The night stayed warm and he decided against a fire as he shed outer clothes and lay down on his packroll, the big Colt at his side. He fell asleep quickly, woke to the sound of raccoons and a distant cry of a cougar and returned to sleep. When morning came he dressed, found a fast-running brook and washed, refilled his canteen, and let the Ovaro drink. He rode north again, found another rise and peered back to see the movement of the trees as the riders took to the saddle again. Fargo guided the Ovaro down onto open land, crossed the thick bromegrass to a stand of black oak and paused to glance behind him again.

The knot of riders had drawn closer, he saw, but they stayed in a line of cottonwoods even though they would make better time on the open land. A furrow touched his brow. There was only one reason for them to stay in the trees. They didn't want to be seen. The furrow stayed on Fargo's brow. The riders were following pretty much in his footsteps as they stayed out of sight. But there was no reason for anyone to be following him, he mused. Or maybe there was, he speculated—two thousand four hundred reasons. It was a lot of money, a sum they had usually exchanged among themselves. They knew he'd come collecting if they didn't pay Charlie Lewis. He'd told them so.

Fargo let the thought hang in his mind. If he wasn't around there'd be no one to come collecting. They put themselves forth as gentlemen horse breeders but arrogance was inbred in them. Besides, he'd seen too many gentlemen change character when real money was involved. Fargo's jaw was set tightly as he sent the Ovaro forward. He continued his casual pace north, moving in and out of the trees, giving those who followed chance to see him. By mid-afternoon he came upon two small towns, hardly more than villages, where he stopped to buy fresh oats for the pinto. No band of riders followed into the town, he noted. At the second village he halted to buy a kerchief at a small general store but again, no group of riders appeared and he rode on as day began to wind down. His followers chose not to move into the open and he found a spot just before darkness descended and made camp. He chose a place at the edge of a line of cottonwoods where anyone watching would see him.

He let the night settle in before he set out his

bedroll and ate two sticks of buffalo jerky from his saddlebag. When the moon rose, he arranged his bedroll to appear as if he were in it, placed his hat at the top and crawled into the nearby brush. The Ovaro moved on a loose tether a few feet away and Fargo settled himself in the brush to wait. He dozed from time to time, confident his wild-creature hearing would wake him at the slightest sound. It did, at the scratching of a trio of weasels, the chatter of a skulk of foxes, even the soft steps of a herd of deer. But nothing else came to him and he woke with the first touch of dawn and quickly pulled his bedroll into the brush. He brought the horse into the brush and trees, put his bedroll onto the horse and moved through the trees at a walk, his eyes scanning the stand of hawthorn across from where he'd camped.

The sun had begun to bathe the land with its warm yellowness when he spotted the motion inside the hawthorns. The riders were moving again but this time their quarry was behind them as Fargo crossed into the hawthorns. He followed, let himself draw a few dozen yards closer and then slowed as the hawthorns came to an end at an expanse of open land. The riders shot forward into the open and across the flat land, spurring their horses into a gallop, and he saw them for the first time, five men in rangehand clothes. One, in the lead, wore a beard and a light tan Stetson and he watched as they reached a stand of red ash and entered the trees again. They immediately slowed their horses and he let them get almost out of sight before he crossed the open land and followed them into the red ash forest.

He watched as they paused a half-dozen times, peering forward to where open land loomed up again. They were plainly searching for someone.

Was it him? Fargo frowned. They could have jumped him where he'd camped but they hadn't. Because they had orders to put more distance between themselves and whoever had hired them? Fargo spied a line of low hills to the east, turned the Ovaro and when the riders were far enough ahead, rode into the hills. He quickly climbed to the high ground and easily spotted the horsemen below. They emerged from tree cover and swung onto a rutted road that led north. The men reined to a halt at one spot, pointed to a place at the side of the road, then spurred the horses into a fast canter. The frown came to Fargo's brow again as he rode along the high ground. It was plain they were trying to pick up a trail and Fargo increased the Ovaro's pace as he peered forward, his view of the land below virtually unobstructed.

He had passed the five riders and moved along a ridge when he glimpsed a lone rider on the road below, some hundred yards ahead of the five horsemen. He spurred the Ovaro forward and felt surprise touch his face as he saw the lone rider was a young woman, brown hair pulled back in a ponytail that streamed out behind her as she rode. She rode unhurriedly, her horse in a slow trot, and she wore a deerskin vest over a blue shirt. He glanced back to the five horsemen and saw them put their horses into a full gallop as they honed in on the hoofprints on the road. His suspicions had been wrong, Fargo realized. It only seemed they might have been following him. It was plain they'd been searching for the young woman and as he watched he saw the girl turn in the saddle, obviously picking up the sound of galloping horses.

He glimpsed a round face with a small, snub nose before she turned back and sent her horse into a gallop. He watched the five horsemen round a curve in the road, see her, and send their horses full-out. Fargo slowed and moved the Ovaro downward out of the low hills as his eyes stayed on the pursuit below. The young woman started to turn toward the low hills, decided against it and continued on the road. But the maneuver had cost her thirty seconds and the five horsemen were gaining on her. He saw the one in the lead veer to his right while two others moved left to come onto the young woman on both sides. She tried to cut west, away from the road, and saw the two riders had come up too close. She had to veer back onto the road and again lost precious time.

Fargo was almost at the bottom of the hills when the horsemen reached her. He saw her draw a pistol, fire two shots that went wild and then they were closing in on her from both sides and behind. One leaned sideways from his saddle, hit her with a roundhouse blow that almost knocked her from her horse. As she struggled to stay on her mount, the bearded one grabbed her one arm, yanked and she went down, landing hard on her back. The men reined up instantly, the bearded one dismounting, first. The young woman was still shaking her head to clear it as he yanked her to her feet and the others dismounted.

"It's a downright shame to have to kill something as pretty as you," the man said in a raspy voice. "So we might as well enjoy ourselves, first."

"That's right," one of the others agreed, gleeful anticipation in his voice. The young woman aimed at kick at the bearded one's groin that, while not a bullseye, nonetheless made him double over.

"Bitch," he cursed in pain as two others grabbed the young woman and threw her to the ground. "Goddamn, you'll pay for that, bitch," the bearded one said. Fargo had reached the bottom of the hill and sent the Ovaro out of the trees onto the road. They hadn't come onto her by accident. There was something more going on here than appeared on the surface. But he wasn't willing to stand by for what he saw and the big Colt was in his hand as he moved into the open.

"That's enough," he said quietly. "Let her go."

The five men turned to him, frowns on each face. "Who the hell are you?" the bearded one bellowed.

"Nobody you know but I'll be taking her," Fargo said.

"Shit you will," the man snarled.

Fargo's eyes were the color of blue ice as they swept the five men. He was too exposed a target in the saddle with no chance to move quickly and he glanced at the edge of the trees only a few feet from him. But they'd draw the minute he tried to dismount, he knew. He gathered himself in the saddle, slipping his boots from the stirrups, and prepared for all hell to break loose.

2

Thigh muscles tensed, Fargo shifted his legs at the same instant he pushed down on the saddle with both hands and vaulted backwards over the horse's rump. He hit the ground on the balls of his feet, the Colt in his hand again as the five men drew their guns. He fired at the nearest one and saw the man clutch his upper arm as he shouted in pain and dropped to one knee. Fargo was already flinging himself in a sideways dive as a hail of bullets erupted. He landed at the edge of the trees, rolled into the brush and came up firing. Another one of the men doubled over, hands clasped to his stomach as he went down. The other three were leveling their fire at the spot where Fargo had disappeared into the trees and he lay flattened on the ground as bullets whizzed over him.

He raised his head just enough to see one of the men reloading and he rolled onto his side, rolled again and drew a bead on the man that finished his reloading. He fired and the man sprawled facedown, his body heaving with the impact of the two heavy slugs. Fargo spun and saw the other two men race into the trees, one on each side of him. He stayed still and suddenly heard the sound of hoofbeats. Glancing through the trees, he saw the young woman racing away on her horse. He swore as she disappeared from sight down the road and he heard the two men closing in on him. They'd have him sandwiched in a cross fire if he stayed. He needed more space to maneuver and he had but moments left. He rose halfway up, tensed powerful leg and shoulder muscles, and dived out of the trees.

He hit the ground, rolled, and leapt to his feet. It took the two men precious seconds to react, rise, and bring their guns around. He had vaulted onto the Ovaro by the time they gathered themselves, flattened down in the saddle as their shots grazed his back and the Ovaro hurtled away. He raced down the road as the two men leaped onto their horses and came after him. Fargo let the Ovaro go some fifty yards before he whirled the pinto in a tight circle and raced back at the two pursuers. He'd already seen that they weren't very good shots and he ducked low in the saddle as the two men veered away from each other to come on both sides of him. Slipping onto the left side of the Ovaro, he fired across the horse's neck with marksmanship few men could command.

The figure bucked in the saddle of the other horse before he sailed into the air with a cascade of red streaming from his chest. Three shots whistled through the air from the other man as Fargo clung to the side of the Ovaro a moment longer, then pulled himself back into the saddle. He reined the Ovaro in, saw the man start to turn his horse around and raised the Colt. The six-gun barked and the man spurred his horse forward, seeming to be untouched and Fargo felt the frown dig into his brow when the man slumped forward and slid from his mount. He landed on the road and lay still, facedown, and Fargo moved closer to the still form. He was about to dismount when he heard the sound of hoofbeats and whirled to see the man he'd wounded in the arm racing away on his horse.

Fargo sent the pinto after the fleeing figure and saw the man leave the road to cut across an open field. He peered at the man, raised the Colt and searched for a shot that would bring him down without killing him. He drew closer to his target, saw a moment to get off a shot, when suddenly he felt himself flying forward over the horse's head. He hit the ground on his back as he heard the Ovaro's yelp of pain. He shook his head for a moment, pulled himself onto one knee, and saw the horse standing with his right foreleg raised off the ground. Only then did he see the deep hole the horse had stepped into while racing at a full gallop.

"Aw, damn," Fargo said as he felt concern and pain sweep over him. He was at the Ovaro's side in seconds, running his hand carefully along the horse's fetlock, cannon bone and tendon. He gingerly touched the knee joint and the chestnut and ran his hand down the horse's leg again. It was already beginning to swell, he saw, and he felt sick to his stomach. "Easy, old friend . . . easy," he murmured, soothing the horse with touch and voice. He had pulled to his feet when he spun, yanked the Colt from its holster as the sound of hoofbeats broke the stillness. But it wasn't the man coming back again. Instead, he saw a dapple-gray gelding with a young woman atop it. But he still held the Colt in his hand as she reined to a halt. "Are you all right?" she asked.

"Yes. Can't say the same for my horse," Fargo said as she swung from the saddle and he saw a tall, slender figure, black riding britches covering narrow hips and long legs, a white blouse that rested lightly on longish but full breasts. She looked at him with the greenest eyes he had ever seen, a patrician face that approached genuine beauty, finely molded lips, delicate cheekbones and a firm chin, all framed by dark brown long hair with a touch of auburn in it. She regarded him with a hint of imperiousness that let her radiate an air of sensuous power.

"I saw you fight off those men. Very impressive. I couldn't come down to help you. I'm not carrying a gun," she said.

"You see anything else?" Fargo asked.

"No, I just came onto it as I reined up on the ridge," she said. "What was that all about?"

"Don't rightly know," Fargo answered, deciding he didn't know enough to say more. "Pack of drygulchers, I guess. They're all over." He turned from her to the Ovaro. "What I need now is a vet."

"There's Doc Sawyer. He's about a mile east of here. He's a good man. I use him all the time. I could fetch him and have him bring his wagon," she said.

"Would you do that? We'd be real grateful to you," Fargo said.

"Of course. I'll be back as fast as I can," she said, pulled herself onto the dapple-gray, breasts gracefully swaying in unison. She left in a clatter of hoofbeats, putting her horse into an instant gallop. Fargo knelt beside the Ovaro. Although the foreleg had already begun to swell, he realized he was lucky not to have to walk the horse. Stroking the horse, he let the soothing touch of his hands keep the Ovaro quiet during the endless wait. But he guessed less than an hour had passed when he saw the forms take shape on the road, the dapple-gray first, then the wagon. As they drew closer he saw that the wagon was an Owensboro dead-axle dray with slatted, thirty-inch high sides, drawn by two horses. The thin, lanky man driving it had spectacles on his nose and sand-colored hair on his head. He pulled the wagon up opposite the Ovaro. "This is Doc Sawyer," the young woman said.

"Thanks for coming, Doc," Fargo said as the veterinarian dropped to the ground and knelt down beside the Ovaro to run his hands carefully over the horse's leg. "I don't think it's a break. I didn't hear anything snap," Fargo offered.

The veterinarian didn't answer until he finished his examination. "Don't see any signs of a break," he said finally. "Let's get him into the wagon." Fargo took the bit and bridle from the horse and left a simple rope halter on him. "Take the saddle off, too. The less weight on him the better," Doc Sawyer said. As Fargo removed the horse's saddle, the veterinarian lowered a wooden ramp at the tail of the wagon and Fargo saw that the wagon floor was covered with a deep layer of straw. With Doc Sawyer helping, he led the Ovaro up into the wagon where the veterinarian tied wide swaths of canvas that were secured at the sides of the wagon around the horse's shoulders and belly. "This pretty much keeps him from moving," the Doc said. "You ride up here with me."

Fargo climbed up onto the wagon seat as the young woman came alongside on the dapple-gray. "I'm Annabelle Davison," she said and he caught a definite air in the way she said it.

"Is that supposed to mean something to me?" he asked.

She laughed, a deep, husky sound. "It does to

most people around here, most people who sail the Mississippi, too," she said.

"Sorry," he shrugged apologetically.

"I see you've never heard of the Davison River-boat Line. We own the largest fleet of riverboats on the Mississippi. My father, rest his soul, founded the line. My brother and I run it now," she said. "You ever traveled by riverboat?"

"Some, but not a lot," he said. "I'm Fargo . . . Skye Fargo. I'm real beholden to you for bringing the Doc."

She tossed him an appraising glance, the green eyes lingering on his chiseled handsomeness. "You just roving, Fargo?" she asked as she rode along-side the wagon.

"I've a job waiting but I'm not due at it for at least a month," he said and saw her eyes continue their appraising examination of him.

"We'll talk more after you tend to your horse, Fargo," she said and rode quietly beside the wagon. Annabelle Davison had a way of saying things that made them sound as if they were an order. She was plainly a very beautiful young woman very much in charge of her world. But he was truly grateful to her for her help. God knows what damage might have been done if he'd had to walk the horse for perhaps miles.

They finally reached Doc Sawyer's place and he saw a rambling spread with barns and stables close together as well as corrals of various sizes where a variety of animals took up space: cows, hogs, horses, dogs, rabbits, and chickens. The wagon halted at a stable where a young man in a long white coat hurried out. "My assistant, Fred," the Doc said and Fargo stood by as Fred helped back the Ovaro from the wagon and into the stable. He followed them inside where Doc Sawyer proceeded on to a more thorough examination, finally calling on Fred to help swatch the pinto's foreleg in thick bandages soaked with an ointment he poured from a heavy clay jar. "My own mixture," the Doc said. "White willow bark compress, balm of gilead and hyssop." Finished the bandaging, the veterinarian straightened up and scratched the Ovaro's forehead. "It's a bad sprain but nothing more. He'll need at last a month's rest. We'll change the poultices every day for two weeks and then keep the leg heavily wrapped. But he'll be fit as ever when it's over. He's a fine horse."

"Write your own ticket, Doc," Fargo said.

"I will," the Doc smiled. "And you'll be needing a horse. Seeing as how you seem partial to pintos, I've a good Tobiano I can rent you. Here, let's take a look at him."

Annabelle Davison followed Fargo and the Doc into the stable where Doc Sawyer took a good, sturdy skewbald from a corner stall, a mostly white pinto with light liver-colored markings. Not quite as powerful in build as his Ovaro, but a good, balanced horse nonetheless. He put his saddle on the Tobiano, took the horse for a ride and returned pleased with the animal's feel. "Very nice. You've a deal, Doc," Fargo said.

"I'll put it on your bill when we're all finished," the veterinarian said and Fargo rode from the stable with Annabelle Davison beside him.

"Seems you're all set," the young woman said.

"Again, I'm real grateful to you, Miss Davison," he said.

"Annabelle, please," she said and he gave a half-bow of his head. "Come back to my place. I'd say you could use a drink and I want to talk to you. It's not far."

"You lead," he said and pulled the Tobiano alongside her horse. She rode well, her body one with the horse, gracefully secure in the saddle. Auburn-tinted hair flowing out behind her, patrician contours of her face coolly contained, he saw again that she possessed a regal loveliness. Fargo saw the beautifully tended fields come into sight first, then the neat white fences of horse corrals that surrounded rich bluegrass. Stables and barns in mint condition came next and then he saw the big white mansion, four columns outside the entranceway, an example of fine, colonial architecture. Beyond the house, he saw lawns leading down to the Mississippi where a big side-wheeler sailed majestically past.

"*The Bayou Queen,*" Annabelle said. "One of our finest riverboats. She's on her way to St. Louis, then to Cairo. *The Bayou Queen* doesn't make a lot of the smaller stops most of the other boats do." She drew to a halt, dismounted and a boy came from the house to take her horse. Fargo followed her into the big house where he found himself in a richly furnished parlor with fine rugs, tall, arched windows hung with thick dark-red drapes and two large sofas. A polished wood cabinet took up part of one wall and Fargo recognized the style as Chippendale. Annabelle opened the cabinet and a shelf came out with glasses and whiskey bottles on it. "What's your pleasure, Fargo?" she asked.

"Bourbon," he said and she smiled as she poured two glasses of whiskey.

"I could have predicted that," she said, sitting down opposite him. She leaned back and her breasts pushed against the white shirt to form two smooth mounds with no hint of a point in either. The whiskey turned out to be wonderfully smooth

33

sour mash that fitted the surroundings. "As you can see, we've inherited Daddy's indulgence in finer things," she said. "I was very impressed by you this morning, Fargo. I'd like you to work for me. I need a man who can handle himself the way you did."

"Work for you as what?"

"A troubleshooter. We have all sorts of problems on the boats, from outright bandits, cardsharps, con men and just plain troublemakers to occasional Indian attacks. You could be very useful. I'd start you out working the boats along this stretch of the river," she said, paused and a half-smile came to touch her lips. "Where I could keep a personal eye on you," she added.

"That sounds like the best part," Fargo said.

Her little half-smile stayed as she shrugged. "You never know," she said. "I'm seldom wrong when I take a fancy to someone."

"This is all very flattering but I told you I've a job ready for me in a month," Fargo said.

"Try my offer meanwhile. I think you'll find it much more interesting than your other job, whatever it is," Annabelle Davison said.

"Besides, troubleshooter's not my line of work. I try to avoid trouble," Fargo smiled. "It doesn't agree with me."

"Your way of avoiding it sure disagreed with those men this morning," she said and Fargo allowed a smile as he shrugged. "Why don't you think more about it?" Annabelle said and looked up as two men entered the manor. "Just who I want you to meet," she said and Fargo got to his feet as the men crossed the room. "This my brother, Garret," she said of the first man. Fargo saw the resemblance at once. The man was tall and lean, and had his sister's patrician features, the same delicate bone structure in his face, the same finely-molded lips, the auburn-tinted hair, a man women would quickly swoon over. But there was a difference. Where Annabelle Davison's face held strength, his edged weakness, where she radiated a touch of arrogance, he transmitted a kind of petulance. She bore their wealth and comfort with imperiousness, he with something bordering on indulgence.

"My pleasure," Fargo said as he clasped the man's hand, found the grip a little flaccid.

"And this is the manager of Davison Riverboats, Barton Spender," Annabelle said, introducing the second man. There was no softness about Barton Spender, Fargo saw at once, as he took in a powerful physique, a strong face with a flattened nose and a head that was almost completely bald. "I've asked Fargo to come work for us," Annabelle said and quickly recounted how he had dispatched the five attackers.

"Quite a story," Garret Davison smiled appreciatively. "But I don't think we need anyone new on the payroll."

"I'd say there are lots of reasons why hiring a man like Fargo would be a wise move. I don't have to spell them out, do I?" Annabelle said and Garret Davison flashed a glance at the manager.

"What do you think, Barton?" he asked.

Barton Spender smiled a slow, affable smile. "You know I never argue with a lady, Garret. I'd like to think more on it," he said. Fargo kept his own smile inside himself. Barton Spender had shown that he was a diplomat or he hadn't the desire to take on Annabelle.

"You don't have to do much thinking," Fargo put in. "I told Miss Annabelle it wasn't likely I'd be taking her offer."

"But you agreed to think about it," Annabelle said to him.

"Did I? If you say so," Fargo nodded.

"We're having a small party tonight, a gathering of neighbors and friends. Would you come, Fargo?" she asked.

"That'll be too fancy an affair for me, I'm afraid," Fargo said.

"We could find something to fit you," Annabelle pressed. His eyes met hers and he found himself wondering if he saw more than a casual invitation in the green orbs.

"Some other time, maybe," he said. "Thanks again for all your help today."

"Come visit tomorrow morning and promise to think hard about my offer," she said.

"Promise," he said with a nod to Garret Davison and the manager. Annabelle walked from the big house with him as he climbed onto the Tobiano. "Your land seems laid out for horses," he remarked.

"Yes, fine horses are a hobby of mine," Annabelle said. "I'll show you some tomorrow, one in particular." She stepped back, green eyes dancing with a very private amusement and he put the horse into a trot. The first lavender shadows of dusk began to settle as he rode from the Davison spread and turned east until the Mississippi was a wide, watery ribbon in front of him.

He turned the horse and rode slowly along the riverbank as dark descended, found a spot to bed down under a cluster of sandbar willow and unsaddled the horse. He ate some of the dried beef strips in his saddlebag as night fell and stayed warm. The moon rose to paint a silver line along the river and he stretched out on his bedroll, watched a riverboat appear and sail downriver. It was a stern–wheeler, the night almost concealing the prosaic reality of smokestacks, ropes and pulleys, and even the sound of the paddlewheel failed to destroy the ethereal quality of the vessel. Aglow in a haze of light, it seemed to move through the night as if it were a beautiful ghostly apparition to finally vanish from sight around a bend in the river.

Fargo lay back and let his thoughts turn to Annabelle Davison. She had shown more than a casual interest in him. Reading signs—all kinds of signs—was his life. The question was how much more of an interest. She could just enjoy toying, all tease and no please. He'd seen that kind before. But then perhaps she was more than that. He'd stay to find out, he decided. He'd nothing planned for the moment. Besides, a beautiful woman should never be left as a question mark. But he'd try to avoid a commitment, though he did owe her a favor, he reflected. He lay back, enjoyed thinking about the possibilities of Annabelle Davison and let sleep slowly embrace him.

When morning came, warm and yellow, he woke, washed at the river's edge and had just finished dressing when another paddle wheeler sailed by, this one smaller, less spectacular and going upriver. He saddled the Tobiano and rode to Doc Sawyer's putting the horse into a trot, canter and gallop to get the feel of the animal. Satisfied, the mount performing well, he reached the veterinarian's to find the Ovaro doing satisfactorily. When his visit ended, he rode on to the Davison manor where Annabelle greeted him at the door looking radiant in a pale green dress with large pearl buttons down the front that set off her auburn-tinted hair. Her appraising smile seemed to have a new edge to it as she studied him and she ushered him into the house where Garret held a mug of coffee.

"Just stopped by to say I haven't decided about taking your offer," Fargo told Annabelle.

"Except that now you have to come aboard, seeing as now I know who you are," she said, eyes flashing and Fargo frowned in question. "An old friend of yours was at our party last night. Sheriff Olsen," Annabelle Davison said.

"Tim Olsen?" Fargo questioned.

"That's right. He's been sheriff in Benton's Landing for the last three years. He said he knew you when he was a deputy in Kansas territory," Annabelle said and Fargo smiled wryly. "He also told me you are the Trailsman. You find what other men never see. You pick up what others pass by. Most men can't read books the way you read trails, Tim said. That's exactly the kind of man I want working for me, Fargo."

"I'd still like to think more on it," Fargo said as Barton Spender entered the room.

"Morning," the man said and focused on Garret. "The *Mary Clark* is due at Benton's Landing in half an hour. We wanted to check out the boiler problem on her, remember?"

"Yes, that's right," Garret Davison said. He took another moment to finish his coffee, started to stand up when the voices came from just outside the front door.

"Wait, you can't just barge in there, missy," a man said.

"Yes, I can," a woman's voice answered and Fargo saw the figure stride into the room. His brows shot upwards as he recognized her at once, the round face and pug nose. She wore the deerskin vest but over a yellow shirt now. It was the young woman who'd fled her attackers as he'd fought with them. She halted and he saw her eyes were a bright, deep blue as she scanned everyone in the room. Her glance passed over him and he was certain she recognized him but she gave no sign of it. "I'm Judy Simmons," she said, her gaze halting at Annabelle.

"Captain Simmons' daughter?" Annabelle said. "I'm sorry about your father's death. It was a terrible accident."

"It wasn't an accident," the young woman said, her round face thrust forward pugnaciously.

"What do you mean, it wasn't an accident? Of course it was," Annabelle said.

"No," Judy Simmons snapped.

"Now, now, I'm afraid you're overwrought, my dear," Garret Davison put in.

"That's what you said to me in St. Louis when I brought this up," Judy Simmons threw back. "Only now I'm more convinced I'm right.

Garret Davison's handsome face took on an air of tolerant patience. "He had been drinking. That was established," he said.

"It was made to look that way," Judy frowned.

Annabelle's voice cut in coolly. "Even if your wild idea is right, which it isn't, why come to us?" she questioned.

"Because everything was fine until you contracted with him to take on all that cargo shipping for you. It was pressure and more pressure, orders to sail twenty-four hours a day, orders from Mister Spender to take on extra men he wanted. It was the same with Captain Thompson and his boat, too much the same," the younger woman said.

"Both Thompson and your Pa were too damn casual about shipping schedules," Barton Spender spoke up.

"I resent your implications, Miss Simmons," Garret Davison said.

"I do too. It was a tragic turn of events. I'm sorry you can't accept that," Annabelle said, her voice turning from cool to annoyed.

"I can't and I won't and I'm going to find out the truth of it," Judy Simmons retorted, then she spun on her heel and strode from the house. Fargo watched as Annabelle, her brother, and Barton Spender stared after her with frowns.

"I'll leave you folks alone for now," Fargo said.

"Wait, we haven't finished," Annabelle said.

"I'll be back," Fargo said and hurried outside. He paused, saw that Judy Simmons had already raced away and he climbed onto the Tobiano. He quickly picked up her hoofprints where she had raced past the gate, the horse digging hooves deep into the ground. He followed, saw she kept the horse full out and picked up where she turned sharply to ride across a field of nettles. He uttered a grunt. She had some trail smarts, enough to know that nettles' tough hardiness let them spring quickly back into place. But not quickly enough to escape his trailsman's eyes and Fargo picked up her path.

One more thing had become clear. There was no doubt left that she had recognized him and plainly expected he'd come after her. Fargo swerved the Tobiano where he saw she had cut right to head down to the river, racing through a cluster of horse chestnut. Her hoofprints didn't turn when she reached the river but disappeared into the water. He slowed when he reached the shoreline and let a small smile come to his lips. She expected he'd be stymied, unable to decide whether she'd gone upriver or down in the water. But his eyes studied the sandy edge of the bank and he uttered a wry snort of satisfaction as he turned the horse upriver. Keeping to the shore let him make better time than riding through the water and he rode with his eyes fixed on the sandy shoreline.

He reined up suddenly as he saw the hoofprints return to shore. Turning the horse into a line of black willow, he rode parallel to the shore until he slowed again. She had dismounted under a wide willow and he moved a dozen yards closer before sending the horse out of the trees. She heard him, spun at once and he saw the pistol in her hand, a double-action, six-shot, Savage and North Navy revolver, a cumbersome piece at best though it fired a mean .36-caliber shell.

"Easy, now. There's no need for that," Fargo said calmly.

"Keep your distance," she said as he swung to the ground.

"I'll do just that," he said, though he edged a step closer as he faced her. He saw the surprise in her eyes as she peered at him.

"How'd you know I came upriver?" Judy Simmons asked.

"You didn't ride out into the river far enough. The water lapped onto the bank where you went upriver," he said.

"You a tracker?" she queried belligerently.

"You could say that," he answered and saw her take a firmer grip on the pistol. "Name's Fargo . . . Skye Fargo."

"You've ten seconds to track yourself out of here," she said. "And don't come back."

"You're setting new records for being ungrateful, honey," Fargo commented and inched a step closer.

"Because of yesterday?"

41

"That's right. I saved your little ass."

"For me or for yourself?" she tossed back.

"Is that why you ran?" he questioned. "Hell, it was plain I wasn't with them."

"You could've been following orders, too," she said. "And from where I just saw you I'd say I was right."

"I only met the Davisons yesterday. My Ovaro was hurt chasing one of those drygulchers. Annabelle Davison was real helpful to me. I was there to say my thanks again," he told her.

But the suspicion stayed in her face. "How sweet," she sniffed. "I'm not in a believing mood." She glowered at him but she had let the barrel of the Savage and North fall away a fraction. He wanted to hear her out and knew there was only one way to do it. She was too full of anger and suspicion to be sweet-talked into trusting him.

"If I wanted you for my own reasons why didn't I come after you?" he asked with calm reasonableness.

She frowned back in thought for a moment and he slid a half step closer. "You said your horse was hurt," she said after a moment.

"So I did. One for you," he conceded with a half-smile. "But I was still only trying to save your ass."

"So you said," she returned.

Some of the anger had gone out of her face and the pistol had lowered a fraction further. "Guess my ten seconds are up," he said and he started to turn and saw her body relax. His next move was fast as a rattler's strike. His arm shot out, a half-backward motion, his hand closing around her wrist. The revolver went off as her finger automatically tightened on the trigger but he had already twisted her wrist and the shot went over his shoulder. He twisted harder and the gun fell from her hand and he flung her away as he scooped the weapon from the ground. She turned, tried to run to her horse but he reached out and grabbed for her. He caught the vest and she pulled out of it and kept running. "I don't want to shoot," Fargo called but she didn't slow a step and he swore under his breath as he raced after her. She was pulling herself onto the horse when he reached her, ducked away from a kick and caught her heel and pulled. She came tumbling from the saddle and landed at his feet.

Fargo glared down at her as, on her hands and knees, she looked up at him. "Pretty damn sure of yourself or pretty damn dumb," he said.

"You said you didn't want to shoot. I took you at your word," she snapped and pushed to her feet.

"Now we can talk," Fargo said, stepping back.

"I'm not telling you anything," she said.

"Why not?"

"So you can run back to the Davisons?"

"No, because I want to hear you out. I'm curious," he said.

"I'll bet you are. You're curious about how much I know," she flung back, anger wrapping itself around her instantly. "Well, I'm not talking. They're not getting off that easy. Maybe you better think about using that gun."

He raised the revolver and watched her deep blue eyes grow wide. They were still wide, emotions racing through them, when he flipped the gun in his hand and gave it to her. "Here, take it. Be a hardhead. Don't take any help," he said, turned and started for the horse. He reached the Tobiano before she called out.

"Wait," she said and he paused, looked back at

43

her. "Why'd you come helping yesterday?" she asked, her face grave.

"Old habit. Didn't like the odds," he said.

"Why'd you come asking now?" she pressed.

"Five bastards came to kill you. There had to be a reason. Maybe you're onto something," Fargo said.

Judy Simmons drew a deep breath and her high, very round breasts lifted. She motioned to him as she sat down on a rock, weariness suddenly flooding her face. He had a chance to study her for the first time without seeing anger or fear in her. Relaxed, she had a surprising winsomeness to her, a lost quality in her eyes that contrasted with her compact, firm figure that seemed to be full of contained energy. "Maybe I am. I think so but I don't know anything much," she said.

"Why don't you tell me what you do know," Fargo said as he sat on the rock beside her.

"No accident," she glowered at once.

He grimaced. "You believe that, but it's not something you know, not yet, anyway," he corrected and she frowned at him. "Tell me the things you know."

"They said he'd been drinking. He didn't drink, not ever. I ought to know that. I was his daughter and I served as mate for years," she said.

"Go on," Fargo nodded.

"He had his own vessel, the *Judy Belle*. You don't need to guess where that name came from. He carried passengers but mostly cargo. Daddy was one of the independents, single boat owners that sail the river."

"As opposed to the Davisons."

"They've a fleet, at least eight boats," Judy said. "There are some six other independents and that many other fleet owners. My Pa is the second captain to be killed on his ship, another accident. It all started some six months ago when the Star Shipping Company contracted to ship all their cargoes on three independent lines. My Pa was one of them."

"Why'd you barge into the Davisons about this?" Fargo questioned.

"Because they were the ones who recommended my Pa's boat and the others to Star Shipping," Judy said.

"That's not much of a connection. It sure doesn't make them party to anybody being killed," Fargo said.

"But there is a connection somewhere. I'm sure of it. Star Shipping practically took over my Pa's boat, they shipped so much stuff. Then after Pa was killed in that phony accident, the *Judy Belle* mysteriously sprang a leak and sank."

"You don't think that was an accident either," Fargo said.

"That's right," Judy Simmons snapped.

"And the other captain?" Fargo queried.

"Willie Thompson. A cargo boom swung loose and hit him, crushed his skull."

"It could happen," Fargo said.

"At midnight, when he went on deck for a look around? A damn strange coincidence the boom comes loose at that moment, especially when you put what happened to Pa with it," Judy returned. "And his boat sank a week later, too. A piece of the bottom fell out. I'm sure it was made to fall out."

"Tell me about your Pa's accident," Fargo said.

"I wasn't aboard. I'd gone visiting a friend for a few days. They said he fell into the paddle wheel and was killed. They found two empty whiskey bottles in his cabin. But he didn't drink, I told

45

you. He wouldn't have fallen into the paddle wheel. It stinks, all of it."

Fargo let thoughts turn in his mind. It was possible to reasonably explain all of it even though Judy insisted her Pa never drank. Maybe there was a part of him she didn't know. Fathers have had secrets from their daughters all too often. It could all have been the long arm of coincidence. Except for one fact that hung in his mind. Five men had hunted down Judy Simmons and attacked her. They had been very real and someone had sent them, he was certain. He shut off his thoughts and returned his gaze to Judy. "You tell anybody else you think your Pa's death was no accident?" he asked.

"Lots of people in lots of places," she said. "Especially after the boat sank."

"Then anybody could've sent those varmints after you. There's no reason to suspect the Davisons. There's no reason to even think the Davisons are involved. Hell, why would they care about a small, independent operator such as your Pa? They've got their own fleets. They certainly don't need any more boats and they're not worried about competition."

"I know, I know, it doesn't add up," she cut in impatiently. "But it all started after they began using our boat and Captain Willie's for their cargo shipping."

"I'd say this Star Shipping Company ought to be checked out," Fargo suggested.

"I tried that. All I came up with was a name and an empty little shed outside Memphis. It seems they turned everything over to the Davisons to handle for them," Judy said.

Fargo frowned in thought before turning to Judy again. "Look, Annabelle Davison wants me to work for her. I think I'll do it. It'll give me a perfect cover to snoop around. Maybe I can turn up something for you. Maybe."

Her hand reached out, covered his. "Would you? God, I'd really appreciate that," she said.

"But I call it the way I find it. That means if I don't find anything you drop it," he said.

"Fair enough," she agreed.

"Where can I find you?" he asked.

"Tonight I'll be at the Inn at Fairlawn. Then I'm on my way to Hannibal to help an old friend of Pa's, Captain Sam Walker. He skippers the *Molly M.* Why don't you come along and meet Sam?"

"I'll see," he said and she got to her feet with him, stood very close, her high, round breasts almost touching his chest.

"Thanks for listening, for being interested. I'm afraid. I see only trouble. I feel it inside," she said.

"You often feel things inside?" he asked.

"Too often. People make fun of me but I'm right nearly every time," she said gravely and he climbed onto the Tobiano. As he left he saw her eyes searching his face, wanting to find hope and trust, but the best she could do was to reserve judgment. He didn't mind. She'd been through a lot. Suspicion was never easy to cast aside. He rode back at an easy canter and let his plans form. He'd walk a tightrope for now. Judy was a strange admixture, feisty and pugnacious and at the same time lost and wounded. He rode on with the feeling that anything he could find to help Judy would help Annabelle Davison, too. She may well be into something she really knew nothing about, he mused. Two good deeds with one stone. He rode on clutching the thought to him.

3

Annabelle was alone when Fargo arrived back at the manor house and she flashed a warm smile at once. "Sorry about that unpleasantness with Judy Simmons," she said.

"I ran into her. She's very upset and doesn't know very much. She admitted that," Fargo said.

"She has some nerve, coming here with her wild accusations," Annabelle said.

"You're right," he said placatingly.

"Let's not talk about her. You think any more about my offer?" she asked.

"Yes. The problem is I don't want to take a job but I do want to help you. I owe you a mighty big favor. If I'd had to walk the Ovaro his leg might have been damaged beyond fixing. So why don't you call on me for whatever you need and let me see what I can do."

Annabelle thought for her moment, the green eyes studying him. "Anything?" she questioned.

"Anything," he said.

"If that's how you'd prefer it," she shrugged. "I've something personal right now. You plainly know horses. Raising and owning horses is a hobby of mine and I've been having a lot of trouble with a big stallion I bought."

"Let's have a look at him," Fargo said.

"This way," Annabelle said and took his arm as she walked from the house with him, a spontaneous yet possessive gesture that was nonetheless pleasant. She led the way to a clean, white stable where a young boy came to the doorway, not more than seventeen, Fargo guessed. "Josh, my exercise boy," Annabelle introduced. "Saddle the gray and bring him out, Josh," she said to the boy. "Remember keep his head tied till you're finished."

"Yes, m'am," the youth said and disappeared into the stable.

"He's that bad?" Fargo queried as Annabelle led him to a round corral with newly painted white fences.

"That bad. We rope him, then tie his head tight to a post while we saddle him. He damn near killed the old man I had working for me. I hired Josh then. He's young and fast on his feet." Annabelle halted and leaned back against the corral fence and her breasts pressed into the green fabric. Her green eyes held a quiet amusement as they studied him when the sound of the stable door interrupted. Fargo turned to see the exercise boy come out barely hanging on to a big, dark gray stallion, at least seventeen hands. Trouble, big trouble, Fargo muttered to himself as he took one look at the horse. This was no horse in fright. This was a horse in fury, his ears laid flat back, his hooves beating a tattoo on the ground, every muscle tensed, his eyes rolled back in rage.

"Hold him, hold him," Annabelle called out. "Get a leg up on him. Show him you're boss."

The boy tried to shorten up on his grip on the reins but the stallion reared and the youth went up in the air. "Get away from him," Fargo said.

"No, keep hold, dammit," Annabelle ordered.

"Get on him. Rein him in from the saddle." The boy leaped, got one hand on the saddle horn and pulled himself onto the horse. He tried to yank back on the reins but the stallion let out a snort of rage, whirled and reared again, then came down hard on his forelegs. The youth pulled on the reins when he should have let himself go forward and cling to the stallion's neck. He was off balance, badly so, when the big horse kicked his rear high in the air. The boy flew from the saddle and landed hard on his back. "Damn," Fargo hissed as he ran forward, certain what was coming next as the stallion whirled and reared, forelegs pawing the air. He came down, sharp hooves smashing onto the figure in front of him.

"Roll, dammit," Annabelle called out but the boy could only half-turn before the hooves struck. Fargo heard his cry of pain over the stallion's wild snort and Fargo's powerful legs propelled him up and forwards as he leaped. He got his arms around the stallion's powerful neck, grasped the horse by the cheekstrap and yanked. He felt himself lifted into the air as the horse spun and reared again but Fargo kept his grip, letting his weight force the horse to the left. Out of the corner of his eye, Fargo saw the boy crawling on his stomach, trying to reach the corral fence. Annabelle's figure cut into his vision as she crossed before him and, arms stretched out, grabbed at the horse's saddle.

"No, get away," Fargo shouted as she pulled herself onto the horse.

"No, dammit. I'll bring him around," Annabelle shouted, trying to get a firm grip on the reins when the stallion whirled as he roared. Fargo felt himself flung into the air as he glimpsed Annabelle sail from the saddle. He managed to stay on his feet as he landed, spun to see

Annabelle on the ground, the stallion charging at her. Lowering his shoulder, Fargo leaped and smashed into the big gray's rump. The horse swerved, roared and spun in a tight circle to come at him. Fargo tensed his leg muscles, went into a half-crouch and counted seconds as the stallion charged. He feinted left and the horse followed, his bulk and thundering speed making it impossible to veer again as Fargo dived to his right.

The horse sped past him as Fargo reached Annabelle, and he half-lifted, half-dragged her to her feet and ran to the corral fence. He heard the stallion's pounding hoofbeats as the horse turned and charged after him. Shaking her head to clear it, Annabelle managed to help Fargo push her through the opening in the fence and fall to the ground on the other side. Fargo stepped back as the stallion hit the fence, reared, pawed at the air before coming down to race back and forth alongside the fence. Fargo saw the boy lying crumpled against a post and he ran to the still figure and pulled the youth clear of further danger. He looked up as Annabelle regained her feet and came toward him.

"He was trampled. Get a Doc," Fargo said.

"Dammit, he should've done better. I worked with him on handling that horse," Annabelle said.

"Not enough. Get the Doc, dammit," Fargo snapped and Annabelle hurried away, went through the stable and he saw her emerge on a chestnut, riding bareback. Fargo stayed on one knee beside the boy, saw that the youth's breath held steady, though blood seeped from his side and chest where the stallion's hooves had struck. When Annabelle returned she had the doctor and his nurse driving a wagon. Fargo helped lift the boy into the back and the doctor drove off at once.

51

"Come by later," he called back and raced the wagon down the road. Fargo straightened up as Annabelle came to stand beside him, her eyes on the stallion that continued to race back and forth inside the corral.

"What do I do with him?" she asked.

"Let him run himself down. He'll be easier to handle then," Fargo said.

"And after that?"

"Sell him. Get rid of him. He's a bad actor. You'll get nothing but trouble from him. He belongs on a farm where they'll only use him as a stud," Fargo said.

"Come inside with me, Fargo," Annabelle said and Fargo went with her as she led the way back to the manor house, up a half-flight of steps and into a large room with a big four-poster bed in the center of it. She turned to him, stood very close to him and in her green eyes he saw an edge of sheepishness. "Thanks to you I'm not lying in the Doc's office," she said as she searched his face. "I guess I wasn't terribly sympathetic to Josh," she said.

"You sure weren't," Fargo agreed.

"I expected more of him. I get annoyed when people don't live up to my expectations," she said.

"That happens when you ask more of people than they can give you," Fargo said. "The kid doesn't have the experience to handle a horse like that. Neither do you."

"I was wrong. I've got to stop being angry when people don't meet my expectations," she admitted, took a step closer and he felt the warmth of her, smelled the strangely exciting mixture of powder and perspiration that seemed to dissipate the coolly assured facade she wore. Her arms lifted, came around his neck and her lips were suddenly against his, lingering, sweet surprise. "I'll bet there are no expectations you couldn't meet," she murmured.

"You could be wrong," he said. "Then you'll be angry again."

"I'd like to find out," she said and he felt her fingers unbuttoning his shirt. He waited, let her peel the shirt from him and watched her eyes move across his hard-muscled torso. He undid his gunbelt, let it slide to the floor as her fingers closed around the buttons of his Levi's. She moved backwards, slid down onto the big four-poster bed as his Levi's fell to the floor. He felt himself responding, growing firm with instant desire and Annabelle's hand clutched at him, closed around his burgeoning maleness still under his shorts. "Oh, my God . . . oh, Jesus," she gasped and he pulled the last of his clothes off as she frantically undid the large pearl buttons down the front of her green dress. Her clothes fell away and he took in a long and lithe but nonetheless voluptuous figure, smooth, very white skin, a narrow waist and the longish breasts very beautifully cupped. He saw why they made no indentations in her garments. Very pale, pink nipples were flat, almost inwardly turned, on tiny areolas of equally pale pink.

A flat abdomen with a tiny little dot in the center led downward to a surprisingly small triangle, flat and almost silky rather than bushy, an almost sleek little v. Just below, long, lovely thighs slid into long, curved, shapely calves, legs that moved as he stared at them, half-parting, then clinging together, the gesture an unmistakable message. Fargo's mouth came down on hers, felt her lips opening at once for him, tongue thrusting forward, demanding, eager and her hands went through his hair as his head moved down to her breasts, drew one longish mound into his mouth. He let his tongue caress the flat light pink nipple, slowly circling, pressing down onto the center until the tiny tip slowly rose, peeked upwards, answered and he heard Annabelle's long shuddering sigh of delight. He pulled gently, caressed the tiny tip, moistened the full-cupped mound and Annabelle's hands moved up and down his muscled back. "Yes, oh, yes, Jesus . . . more, more," she breathed and Fargo let his hand move slowly across the flat abdomen, down to the sleek little v and pressed down on a surprisingly soft mound.

Annabelle's hips lifted and her long thighs fell open, her body urging, demanding, words of the flesh, and her hand came down, found his throbbing maleness and she uttered a half-scream of delight, pulled on him. "Take me . . . God, take me," she murmured and swerved hips, legs, torso, urgent wanting in her every turn and twist. He brought himself to her, rested at the sequacious opening and felt all her wonderful moistness. "Yes, yes, oh, now, now," Annabelle almost screamed and he pushed forward, sliding through the warm, wonderful welcome, surrounded at once by exploding sensation. Her long thighs rose, clasped around him as he pressed her rear with his hands and she was lifting, bucking, surging, yet everything done with a tight focused energy that added new dimensions to ecstacy. He felt her flowing around him as she moved, her legs only an added pleasure to the inner embrace, that caress of all caresses. He let her set her own pace, a slow dance of passion that gathered speed until there was only the gasping, breathing rush of togetherness, ecstacy surrounding ecstacy, sensuality consuming itself.

Suddenly, she let out a sharp cry and he felt her long body stiffen, thighs squeeze hard and she pulled his mouth down to one pale pink nipple. "I'm . . . I'm coming, oh, Jesus, now, now . . . iiii-ieeee . . ." Annabelle screamed as she quivered against him, a vise of passion and he heard his own cry as he exploded with her and the world fell away. But eternity dissolved, the world somehow returning and he heard her long sigh of reluctance as she sank down limply beneath him. He lay with her and slowly, her long legs moved, sliding up and down against his thighs, a motion both languid yet quietly erotic until finally she lay still, pressed tightly against him.

Finally, he slid from her and lay beside her as she brought one leg up over his groin. Half-turned, she lifted her head and he saw her green eyes peering at him with a kind of satisfied smugness. "I was right," she said.

"About what?" he said with a frown.

"About you living up to expectations. About not being disappointed," she said.

"We try," he remarked.

"I think we're going to have a very good time together, Fargo," she said.

"You don't hold back any, I'll say that," he commented.

"Not when I want something."

"And you always get what you want?" Fargo queried.

"Yes," she said and there was no arrogance in her tone, only a cold certainty. Annabelle, he decided, could be an iron fist inside a velvet glove. She rose, swung from the big bed, a slow, supple movement, legs, breasts, arms, all moving smoothly together as she slipped on the dress. "I expect Garret and Barton will be back soon," she said. "I like to keep my private life private."

"Why not?" Fargo said as he pulled on clothes. She waited outside for him as he finished dressing and took his arm when he came out. "I have to spend the next day or two going over the books with Garret," she said.

"I'll wander for a few days," Fargo said.

"Not longer. I'll be waiting," Annabelle said.

"Garret run the business?" Fargo asked.

"He oversees it, with Barton Spender's help," she said.

"What's that mean exactly?" Fargo pressed.

A diffident smile touched her lips. "It means Daddy left the Davison line to me. He never felt Garret was strong enough to run the fleet," she said. "I get a monthly report from Garret."

"But you let him run things."

"I detest the boring details of running a business. But I hold the reins," Annabelle added and walked with Fargo to the Tobiano, pressed her lips to his for a moment. "See you in two days," she said. "Then we'll go visit one of my biggest riverboats. I want you to get the feel of things." She paused. "That includes me," she said, green eyes dancing.

"Count on it," Fargo said as he climbed onto the horse and rode from the manicured fields of the property. He turned the horse to the river and rode north along the Mississippi. There was still light left in the day when he reached Benton's Landing where he saw two small riverboats and an ark tied up at the long wharfs. He rode past, turned into the waterfront town and finally halted before the clapboard building with the word SHER-IFF on the window. He dismounted, went into the building and saw Tim Olson stand up from behind a battered wood desk.

"Skye Fargo, you old son of a gun," the sheriff said with a broad grin cracking his leathered face. "Annabelle Davison told me you were around. I wondered if you'd come visiting."

"Wouldn't be this close and not stop by," Fargo said and Tim Olson saw him take in the three barred cells at the rear of the room. "You need that much jail space here?" Fargo asked.

"When I get a drunken crew of riverboat men. I keep them locked up till they sober up. That's about the size of the trouble we get around here, not that I'm complaining," Tim Olson said.

"I heard there's been some other kind of trouble lately," Fargo ventured.

"You've been talking to Judy Simmons," the sheriff said and Fargo half-shrugged an admission. "She came to see me. But all she has is a pack of suspicions, the talk of a very upset young woman. Her throwing accusations at the Davisons is pretty damn thin stuff."

"You know the Davisons well, Tim?" Fargo questioned.

"I know they've plenty of money and Annabelle runs a tight ship," the sheriff said.

"I hear there was another captain who was suddenly killed. His boat sank soon after too," Fargo said.

"I know, Captain Willie Thompson. But accidents happen all the time on the river. A pair of them isn't that unusual," the sheriff said.

"I was there when five varmints figured to enjoy her and then kill her," Fargo said. "They had to have a reason."

"Why does a pack of coyotes go after a chicken? They only need one reason," Tim Olson said.

57

Fargo nodded, unable to disagree. "But what if there was another reason," he said.

"Find it. Give me something to go on. You might come up with something I couldn't. I'm too well-known up and down this part of the river," the sheriff said. "It'll be like old times," he added. Fargo kept the smile to himself. Annabelle wanted him to troubleshoot for her. Judy wanted him to help her. Now Tim Olson urged him to investigate. Everyone with their own reasons for the same thing. Could he satisfy any of them, he wondered. But he was intrigued by the unanswered.

"Why not?" he said to the sheriff who broke out a bottle of bourbon and they toasted to old times and old acquaintances until dusk began to slide into night. "I'll be in touch, Tim," Fargo said.

"Hard facts only for me. I can't do with less," Tim Olson called out as Fargo climbed onto his horse and rode on. He rode north again, veered inland some from the river and darkness held the land when he reached the town, the moon already climbing high into the sky. He found the Fairlawn Inn, a modest structure once white but now a streaked gray. An old man at the front hallway looked up as Fargo entered.

"Looking for a Judy Simmons. I understand she might be here," Fargo said.

"Room four, down the hall," the man said. "We don't allow two in a room less'n you can prove you're married folk."

"Just paying a visit," Fargo said and hurried down a dim hallway to the last door. He knocked and half-whispered against the door. "It's me, Fargo," he said. "You awake?"

He heard the sounds from inside the room and the door opened. She was fully dressed, white shirt hanging loose over riding britches. "Yes, I can't sleep," she said, her face troubled. "Something's wrong."

"What do you mean?" Fargo asked.

"On the *Molly M.* With Captain Sam. I know it. I feel it. There's trouble," Judy said.

"Maybe your imagination is just working overtime," Fargo said.

"No." She spit out the word almost savagely. "There's trouble. I'm going to him tonight . . . now." She spun, started to pick up her things and he reached out, putting a hand on her arm.

"Simmer down. Think again," he said.

"My horse is in the stable next door," she said, brushing past him to stride from the room, compact rear swinging with her every step. He followed, waiting outside until she reappeared on her horse and he swung onto the Tobiano.

"I'll go with you," he said.

"Why? You think I'm imagining things," she sniffed, sounding hurt.

"Guess I'll find out," he said and rode beside her as she put her horse into a fast canter. She rode in silence, a fierce concentration in her face, and she stayed on the flat land near the river. The moon had reached the midnight sky when they reached Hannibal. The Mississippi sparkled in the moonlight and Fargo took in the dark outlines of riverboats moored to the long wharves. Judy rode to the last wharf, where one of the smaller boats nestled against the dock. There she swung from her horse and strode onto the dark deck. Fargo dropped the Tobiano's reins over a mooring bollard and followed her onto the narrow deck.

"His quarters are right below the pilothouse," Judy said as she hurried along the deck. She had reached amidships, Fargo on her heels, when he heard the sudden splash of water, a heavy, thudding sound. "Captain Sam," Judy cried out as she started to run. Fargo heard the sound of footsteps running on the other side of the vessel, raced past Judy and across the low stern deck alongside the still sternwheel. He skidded onto the starboard deck just in time to see the body disappearing under the surface of the water. A quick glance forward let him see two men racing to the bow of the boat.

"Damn," he swore, as he knew he had only one choice. He pulled off his boots and shed his jacket then dived over the side and into the water. He went down where he'd seen the body sink, kicked his legs hard as he dove straight with his arms outstretched. It was too dark to see but his left hand struck against something and he closed it, felt the wool of a garment. He struck out deeper, got one arm around the body and used all his strength to propel himself upwards. He saw he was but a few feet from the side of the riverboat as he broke the surface and Judy ran toward him, dropped to her knees on the deck as he reached the vessel. She grasped hold of the man, held him as Fargo pulled himself out of the water and reached down to pull the limp form upwards, grateful for the less than a foot deck clearance common to the riverboats.

"Captain Sam, can you hear me?" Judy said as she bent over the limp form now on the deck. "He's breathing," she said and Fargo nodded. The man suddenly made a sound, a rasping breath of air, then a moan and his eyelids fluttered. "Oh, thank God, he's coming around," Judy said. Fargo stayed on one knee beside her and noticed for the first time that the man had only long johns over his thin body. He pulled his eyelids open, stared upwards. "It's me, Judy Simmons. You're all right, Sam," she said.

Captain Sam moved his lips before he found his voice. "I was asleep in my cabin," he breathed. "They gagged me before they brought me out on the deck."

"You'll be all right," Judy said. "Here, I'll help you sit up."

"No, Jesus. . ." the man said, pain and fear in his voice. "They broke my legs. Used a bat."

"Goddamn," Fargo bit out. "Then they dragged you out on deck." The Captain nodded as he groaned again in pain. "They took the gag off you before they threw you in," Fargo said and Captain Sam nodded again.

"Why'd they do that?" Judy frowned.

"They knew he'd wash up ashore downriver someplace. If he were found with a gag on him it'd blow apart being an accident," Fargo said.

"Wouldn't two broken legs do that, too?" Judy asked.

"No. Probably nobody'd notice his legs were broken and if they did it'd be chalked up to his having hit a rock somewhere along the way," Fargo answered.

"Another accident that wasn't an accident," Judy said. "You believe me now?"

"It sure seems that something's going on," Fargo said. "But this doesn't say who, what or why so I wouldn't go finger pointing." Judy set her lips together but conceded with a nod. "Now let's get the Captain here to a Doc."

"Wake the men in the crew quarters," the Captain said between groans of pain.

"I'll do it. I know where it is," Judy said and hurried away. Fargo stayed beside Captain Sam and saw the pain in the man's face.

"You get a look at the bastards?" he asked.

"Just blurred faces. It was dark," the Captain said. "One had a beard, that I remember."

"Everything helps," Fargo said and rose to his feet as Judy returned, four crewmen wearing only trousers behind her.

"There's a doctor in Hannibal. Someone went to fetch him," Judy said.

"Jesus, Captain Sam, we didn't hear a thing," an older crewman said with a blanket under his arm. "We'll get this around you," he said and Fargo lent a hand as the men carefully lifted the Captain, who cried out in pain. Captain Sam was placed on the blanket and carried from the vessel when the doctor arrived.

"I'm going to stay aboard and look after things for him," Judy said.

"I want a look in his cabin," Fargo said and Judy led the way to a cramped but neat area. She lighted a kerosene lamp and Fargo surveyed the room. "Nothing touched," Fargo said. "Just wanted to be sure it wasn't robbery."

"I could've told you that," Judy sniffed.

"You've a real talent for jumping to conclusions," Fargo said. "I like to check the facts."

"I wasn't imagining trouble, was I?" she reminded him with a touch of smugness.

"No, you weren't," he admitted. "But getting a flash isn't the same as nailing down facts."

"What are you going to do now?" she said as he started back along the deck.

"See if I can pick up a trail," Fargo said. He swung from the boat onto the wharf and led the Tobiano away as Judy turned back into the cabin. The two would-be killers had horses waiting, Fargo was certain. But it was far too dark to pick up tracks and he led the horse under a black willow at the end of the wharves, took down his bedrolls and shed his clothes. He stretched out and made the most of the remaining hours of the night. But he was awake and dressed when the first pink-gray light of dawn touched the sky. He walked slowly along the wharf where the *Molly M.* lay tied, halted when he found the two sets of footprints in the soil alongside the wharf. He followed and found the hoofprints of two horses a hundred yards back under a box elder. The hoofprints told their own story at once. They led inland, hoofmarks dug deep into the ground, both horses in a hard gallop.

Fargo followed the trail, certain he had the right set of prints. He was even more certain when, after a half mile, the hoofprints no longer dug deep into the earth. The riders had slowed after putting distance between themselves and the waterfront. The sun rose, heating the land at once and Fargo followed the tracks as they led further inland, along a rutted roadway and a line of hawthorn. He reined up suddenly, his eyes reading the ground. The two horses had come to a halt and then he saw the third set of hoofprints appear, coming in from the south. A third horseman had met with them and again Fargo's eyes read the signs as other men read books.

The third horseman had met with the first two and then turned away, leaving his hoofprints going southeast. Fargo's eyes were narrowed as he scanned the soil ahead and saw the first two riders had gone on, now moving northwest. He followed and after another thousand yards halted where the two riders had stopped beside a line of hawthorn. They'd dismounted and stretched out on the ground to rest before going on. Fargo swung from the Tobiano and knelt down where the trail of their hoofprints went on again. He pressed his fingers into the earth and smiled grimly. The prints were still warm, their edges still clean. The two riders were not more than a few hours ahead of him and he put the horse into a trot. The trail led over a small hill into good, green country, the prints growing more difficult to spot. But the bromegrass was deep enough and he was able to pick up the trail. The two men were walking their horses with unhurried confidence. They entered a small forest of bitternut and stayed out of the sun's heat and Fargo swore silently. The overgrown forest floor obscured the clarity of hoofprints though he was sure they weren't clever enough to have figured on that.

He slowed and took his eyes from the ground, let his gaze go to the low branches of the trees. It took him a few minutes but he finally picked up the leaves still turned back, new twigs broken off where the horses had brushed against them. The two riders emerged from the bitternut a half-mile on and Fargo went into a trot again as he followed the prints over a low rise, through a smattering of red ash and yanked the horse to a halt. Just beyond the trees a small pond glistened in the sun and alongside, two horses drank from the clear blue water. Two men were just recapping their canteens. One sported a black beard.

Fargo gave a grim snort as he swung from the saddle and took the big Henry from its rifle case.

4

Staying alongside the trunk of a thick tree, Fargo dropped to one knee, sighted along the barrel of the rifle and fired a single shot. A shower of spray flew into the air as the bullet hit the water at the very edge of the pond. Both men whirled, dropped into a half-crouch as they drew their guns, their eyes peering into the stand of red ash. Fargo moved halfway behind the tree, the rifle at his shoulder. "That was a warning, not a miss. The next one goes into somebody's gut. Drop your guns," Fargo called. The two men stayed in their half-crouched positions as they scanned the trees. Fargo's finger tightened on the trigger of the rifle again and the shot slammed into the ground at the edge of the bearded man's foot. "Last chance," he said. "Drop the guns." He glanced at the other man and saw a wide face with small eyes that seemed too far apart.

The men exchanged quick glances of uncertainty and the bearded one slowly let his gun drop from his hand. The small-eyed one hesitated another half-second before dropping his gun and straightening up. Fargo stepped from the trees, the big Henry trained on the two men. "Who the hell are you, mister?" the bearded one rasped.

"I'm asking the questions," Fargo said. "Why'd you try to kill the captain?"

"We don't know what you're talking about," the bearded one said.

"I trailed you from Hannibal," Fargo said.

"You trailed wrong," the other one growled.

"I don't think so. You met somebody. Who was it?" Fargo said.

"Nobody," the bearded one said.

Fargo gave them a look of tolerance. "Don't make it harder for yourselves. I'm giving you a chance to cooperate. You could get a reduced sentence."

"For what? We didn't do anything. You've got the wrong men," the one with the beady eyes answered.

"Then you boys won't mind coming back with me," Fargo said. "We'll let Captain Sam have another look at you."

The two men exchanged quick glances again. "You're all wrong about us, mister," the bearded one said.

"I've been wrong before. Let's find out. Get your horses, real nice and slow," Fargo said. The two men turned to their horses and the bearded one reached his, stopped, his body toward the saddle. "Don't do anything stupid," Fargo said quietly. The man stayed in place, slowly reached up to take hold of the saddle horn just as the other one spun, drew the knife from inside his shirt and threw it, all in one quick motion. Fargo ducked and twisted as the knife hurtled at him, fired off a shot but saw it go wide and the knife grazed his arm. Both men dived for their guns as Fargo brought the rifle up again. He saw the bearded one reach his gun first and the big Henry sounded again. The man, in a half-crouch, never got the revolver up as the shot slammed into him. He flew backwards, hit the horse, who skittered away, and the man fell to the ground in a stain of red.

But Fargo dived sideways as the wide-faced man reached his gun and came up firing. Rolling across the ground as bullets slammed into the dirt a fraction of an inch from him, Fargo managed to fire the big Henry with a low trajectory of shots. "Ow, Jesus," he heard the man cry out in pain, rolled again and saw the man sprawled on the ground, holding one hand to his calf.

"Drop it," Fargo ordered but the man, his eyes blazing with a combination of fury and fear, brought the revolver up again.

"Shit I will, you bastard," the man swore and Fargo fired again, two shots, and the figure bucked upwards before collapsing to twitch for a moment and then go rigid. Fargo rose, all too aware of how close death had come to him, and walked to where the two horses stood beside one another. He opened the saddlebag of the nearest, rummaged inside and brought his hand out clutching a handful of twenty-dollar bills wrapped together with twine. Counting the money, he found it came to three hundred dollars, all in brand-new crisp bills.

He stepped to the second horse and found another three hundred dollars in its saddlebag, also made up of brand-new crisp bills. One thing had been answered, Fargo grunted. The rider they had met had been delivering their payoff, crisp new bills but blood money nonetheless. Fargo put the bills into his jacket pocket, swung onto the Tobiano and turned the horse south toward Hannibal. Someone would be along in time to find the bodies and take the horses, he knew and he set a steady pace as he rode southward. The sun was in the afternoon sky when he reached the riverboat alongside the last wharf. The compact figure came to the rail at once and Fargo rested his gaze on the captain's cap with the gold braid atop Judy's light-brown hair. It gave her an added perkiness, he decided.

"Captain Sam's idea," Judy said as Fargo dismounted and stepped onto the boat.

"He made you skipper?" Fargo asked in surprise.

"He knew I could handle the job and he said I was the only one he could trust," Judy answered a touch defiantly.

"I'd guess this makes you the first and only woman riverboat skipper on the Mississippi," Fargo said.

"Yes," she said, her chin lifting.

"How is Captain Sam?" Fargo asked.

"In splints at Doc's place. It'll be months before he can walk," Judy said. "You find anything?"

"The two varmints who tried to kill him," Fargo said and Judy's eyes widened. "But I never got a chance to bring them back. They insisted on putting up a fight." He took the crisp new bills from his jacket and handed them to her. "This is what they were paid for the job. Give it to Captain Sam. It'll pay his doctor bills."

"Yes, it will," Judy said as she put the money in a pocket. "Now what?"

"I've been thinking about Star Shipping," Fargo said.

"We're waiting for another shipment from them today to go with the rest we've on board. When it comes we sail downriver to Memphis."

"Let me have a look at what you have now," Fargo said and Judy led the way to where the forward deck was covered with big, four-stave barrels. "What's inside these?" he asked.

"The bills of lading all say Borax," Judy said.

"Anybody ever check?"

"Yes. After Pa was killed I took the top off six of the barrels on the *Judy Belle* and poked around inside them with a long pole. Didn't find anything but borax," Judy said.

Fargo looked at the floor of the deck and saw the fine, white powdery residue. "Some of it leaks out, I see," he commented.

"Barrels aren't that tight. There's bound to be some leakage," Judy said.

Fargo's gaze stayed on the barrels. "Borax isn't valuable enough for killing and sinking boats," he thought aloud.

"Pa's boat made seven trips loaded with the borax barrels before he was killed and the boat sunk. Same with Captain Willie and this here load makes the sixth shipment for the *Molly M.* I say it's a connection," Judy insisted.

"And maybe it only seems that way. Maybe there's no connection to the borax at all. Maybe it's something else," Fargo said.

"Such as?"

"Damned if I know," Fargo admitted.

"A man came aboard a week before Pa was killed and the *Judy Belle* sunk. He said he was from Star Shipping and he inspected the way we had the barrels stored. He especially checked out how much leakage of powder there was on the cargo deck. I remember Captain Willie saying a man from Star Shipping had visited his ship too," Judy recalled.

"What about the *Molly M.*"

"I'll ask Captain Sam," she said.

"I want to know more about Star Shipping. Have you a log from your Pa's ship and from Captain Willie's?" Fargo asked.

"Pa's log floated to the surface. The mate had Captain Willie's. They're both at the dockmaster's office in Memphis," Judy said.

"I might just go get them," Fargo said. "Meanwhile, I'm going back to check on my Ovaro at the vet's."

"And Annabelle Davison?" Judy slid out, a feline edge to her tone.

"She might know something that'll help," Fargo said evenly and saw Judy's pug nose crinkle. "Where do I catch up to you?" he questioned.

"Soon as the shipment's here we sail downriver, Flats Corners, first, then St. Louis to pick up boiler wood. We stop next at Chester, Cape Girardeau, then Cairo, down along Tennessee to Osceola and then Memphis."

"I'll find you," Fargo said and stepped from the boat onto the wharf.

"Wait," Judy called, followed to stop close to him, her eyes searching his face. "Thanks for believing in me," she said.

"It's getting easier," he conceded.

"Then thanks for helping," she said, reached up and her mouth was against his, her body pressed to him and he felt more than one twinge of surprise. He hadn't expected her compact, chunky body to be so soft. "So you'll remember who you're helping," she said, drawing back.

"Thanks," he said dryly and swung onto the Tobiano. He rode away aware of her eyes watching him. Judy Simmons was an intriguing little package, he reflected. She clung to suspicions, easily dismissed logic, yet she possessed strange insights, inner premonitions that were perhaps a special kind of wisdom. She stayed in his thoughts as he set a steady pace, found a spot to bed down when night came and in the morning he rode to Doc

Sawyer's place. He was pleased at what he found, the Ovaro outside with a small covering of bandages and he spent an hour with the horse, giving him a light rubdown with the body brush from his saddlebag. It was late morning when he rode on to arrive at the Davison place, the Mississippi flowing behind the well-manicured property.

Barton Spender, his almost bald head glistening in the sun, stood at a small table where a line of employees received their monthly pay, ranch hands, stable boys, servants, and groomers. Barton Spender paid each man out of a small iron cash box and Fargo felt his hands tighten on the reins. Each man received his pay in crisp brand-new bills. Fargo kept the horse going until he halted at the manor house and swung to the ground. Garret Davison met him at the door.

"Come in, Fargo. Annabelle ought to be back soon. She's out working a new filly," Garret said. "I'll be taking the *Delta Belle* to New Orleans in a few minutes."

"Business?" Fargo said.

"Business and pleasure," Garret Davison said.

"I think there's something you ought to hear before you go," Fargo said. "Judy Simmons has hold of something."

Garret Davison's handsome face went blank. "What do you mean?" he asked cautiously.

"Her Pa's death may not have been an accident," Fargo said. "I came onto some things that make me think it wasn't. I was there when two hired killers tried to do in Sam Walker of the *Molly M.*"

Garret Davison's tongue came out to wet his suddenly dry lips. "You can't think that we had anything to do with that," he said.

"Didn't say that, but maybe there's a lot going

on you don't know about," Fargo said. "Your business manager, Barton Spender, how long has he been with you?"

"At least five years. Why?" Garret Davison frowned.

"Just wondered. The two killers were paid off with brand-new money. I just noticed Spender paying the help with brand-new money."

"A coincidence, that's all," Garret Davison said.

"Maybe," Fargo allowed.

"Of course that's what it is. Barton's a friend as well as an associate. He wouldn't be involved in anything. It's quite preposterous," Garret said and Fargo saw that his left hand was shaking.

"Didn't mean to upset you," Fargo remarked calmly.

"Well, you certainly did. There has to be another explanation for whatever you found," Garret said, licking his lips again.

"Maybe you'd like to tell me what this is all about," the voice cut in and Fargo turned to see Annabelle in the doorway, her tall figure clothed in a deep blue, one-piece riding outfit that gave her an even longer, leaner look.

"Go on, tell her what you told me," Garret said accusingly.

"Please do," Annabelle said, moving into the room, her green eyes on Fargo. He gave a half-shrug and told her what had happened, recounting the events in greater detail than he had for Garret. When he finished, Annabelle's thin eyebrows held a faintly disdainful arch.

"First, Garret's absolutely right about Barton and the new money. Perhaps it's only natural for you to wonder about that but Barton isn't the only one who pays his men with new money. Mr.

Hodges at the bank in Benton's Landing can tell you that," she said.

"Maybe you're right but that still leaves a picture of murder and attempted murder," Fargo said.

Garret interrupted, his voice rising in pitch. "Well, we've nothing to do with that. I won't listen to any more of this innuendo. Besides, I've got to go to New Orleans," he said and strode across the room to the door where he halted as Annabelle's voice sounded, her tone icily sharp.

"Wait," she snapped. "I thought Barton was going to New Orleans."

Barton threw a glance at her that was uneasy and uncomfortable. "It'll be best if I go," he said and hurried from the house, almost darting out the door. Fargo's eyes went to Annabelle and saw the cold fury in her face.

"He sure upsets easily," Fargo remarked.

"Yes. That's why Daddy left the business to me. Garret's much too sensitive for his own good. And he's loyal. That's why it upset him so that you implied Barton was involved in something," Annabelle said.

"What do you know about this Star Shipping outfit?" Fargo asked.

"Not much. I told you, I leave the details of running the company to Garret and Barton. Stay here. I want to talk to Barton and I'll send him in to see you," she said and strode from the house. Fargo watched her go and sidled up to one of the tall, arched windows. He saw Annabelle outside with Barton Spender, her face tight with anger but the closed window prevented her words from reaching him.

Fargo turned away as thoughts leapfrogged through his mind. Garret Davison had grown much too agitated, the weakness in him quickly apparent. Yet there had been more than weakness, his nervousness entirely too defensive. As for Annabelle, Fargo felt his first thoughts about her being reinforced. There was perhaps a lot more going on around her than she knew. Barton Spender came into the room and Fargo broke off thoughts.

"I hear you're pretty damn quick at jumping to conclusions, Fargo," the man said, his voice surly.

"Maybe," Fargo allowed. "Tell me about Star Shipping."

"Not much to tell. Never met any of the bosses. They sent us orders and payment by mail. We told them we couldn't handle that much cargo and they asked us to ship it for them, for extra cost, of course. We arranged with some of the small cargo riverboats to take their stuff."

"Such as Captain Thompson, Judy Simmons's Pa and Captain Walker of the *Molly M.*," Fargo said and Barton Spender nodded.

"That's all there was to it. We just shipped their stuff for them on the cargo boats," Spender said.

"Only it seems there's a lot more to it," Fargo said.

"Not for us," Barton Spender glowered. "Got any more questions?"

"Not for now," Fargo said and the man strode toward the door.

"Next time don't go jumping to conclusions," he tossed back.

"I'll try to remember that," Fargo said as he made a mental note to stop at the Benton's Landing bank and ask how many people used brand-new money regularly. And who, Fargo added. He walked from the house and met Annabelle outside at the columns.

"Was just coming in to get you," she said. "Get your answers?"

"Not many. It seems Star Shipping is a kind of shadowy outfit," Fargo said.

"But it may not have a thing to do with whatever else is going on. Judy Simmons makes that connection and it doesn't hold," Annabelle said.

"Two Captains killed, their boats sunk, a third almost killed and the attempts on her life, all after Star Shipping began sending their stuff. You've got to wonder," Fargo said.

"It could just be a chain of coincidences. These small independent cargo riverboats are known to take on all kinds of cargo. I'd forget about Star Shipping and look somewhere else," Annabelle said.

Fargo shrugged and his gaze went to the stable as the door opened and Barton Spender came out on a big gelding and put the horse into a gallop as he raced away. "He's in a sudden hurry," Fargo commented.

"My orders," Annabelle said. "I told him to catch up to the *River Belle* at one of her stops and bring Garret back." She paused and saw Fargo's frown of surprise. "On his last trip to New Orleans, Garret got into a fight with a group of very rough, unsavory characters. He could have been killed. I don't want that to happen again and I know he's going back to prove he's not afraid to go back."

"That doesn't sound like somebody weak," Fargo said.

"But it is. The weak have to keep showing they're not weak, to the world and to themselves. It's very typical behavior," she said.

"Seems you let him run the company but you do a lot of mothering," Fargo said.

"Only when I feel I must," she said. "But let's talk about more pleasant things, such as you and

I. Meet me at Benton's Landing in two hours. One of our other big boats is landing there, the *Moonlight Rose*. I want you to have a look around it, get the feel of it."

"Seeing as how I'll be troubleshooting aboard your boats?" Fargo smiled and she gave a sheepish shrug. "All right, but still no promises," he said and she brushed his cheek with her lips as he halted at the Tobiano. "By the way, how's your exercise boy?" Fargo asked as he mounted.

"I suppose he's going to be all right," Annabelle said.

"You suppose?"

"I haven't had time to go check but the Doc would have told me if there was a problem," Annabelle said and hurried back to the house. Fargo gave a little grunt inside himself. She was a mixture of opposites. She could be all warmth and understanding and almost inconsiderate. He put the horse into a leisurely trot, saw the sun was moving down the afternoon sky, and when he reached the waterfront town he stopped in to visit Tim Olson. He told the sheriff what he'd come across during his visit to Judy and Tim frowned into space when he finished.

"She might be onto something but I still don't see any connection to the Davisons," he said.

"What do you know about Barton Spender?" Fargo asked.

"He seems to be a good manager for them. Never heard anything bad about him," the sheriff said.

"And Garret Davison?" Fargo questioned.

"He's always been too much of a playboy for my tastes," Tim Olson said. "Annabelle's had trouble keeping a tight rein on him but she seems to manage."

"I'm wondering if it's as tight as she thinks," Fargo said.

"Maybe it isn't but how does that fit in with what you're telling me looks like murder and the sinking of riverboats?" the sheriff said.

"It doesn't, not yet, anyway," Fargo admitted.

"And you've nothing hard enough for me to act," Tim Olson said. "Keep digging."

"Count on it," Fargo said.

"I hope Judy Simmons appreciates your help," Tim said.

"I think maybe she's not the only one I'm helping," Fargo said as he left for his next stop, the Benton's Landing Bank. The bank president proved to be an easy-to-see, genial man who answered questions openly.

"Who uses new money? Barton Spender for the Davison outfit. Ray Owens up in Bowling Green, Tom Williston here in Benton's Landing and a few shopkeepers who like the idea. Of course, folks can bring in new money from other banks," the bank president said.

"Thanks for your time," Fargo nodded and a furrow dug into his brow as he rode back to the river. His answer hadn't pinpointed Barton Spender but it hadn't absolved him entirely, either. The others had no connection to the riverboats or Star Shipping. But he put aside further speculation as he reached the wharf and saw Annabelle waiting, looking coolly lovely in the one-piece, deep blue outfit. She stood framed against the big riverboat behind her, a side-wheeler, three decks, the lines of the vessel a strange mixture of its own.

"The *Moonlight Rose*," Annabelle said proudly. "Isn't she beautiful?"

"She is," Fargo said as his eyes moved slowly over the riverboat which, for its essentially ungainly shape, somehow conveyed delicacy, dignity, and beauty. The deckwork filigree echoed the grace of the vessel's long lines, its bulk somehow lessened by the elegance of the superstructure carving. Even the twin iron chimneys, which he knew were never called funnels by rivermen, rose up almost a hundred feet adorned with graceful ironwork. Fargo dismounted and Annabelle took his arm as she led him to the riverboat in the gathering dusk.

"She's built out of pine instead of oak—timbers, bulkheads, decks, floors, upper structure, all of pine instead of oak. Oak's stronger but pine is much lighter. With pine, we can have a draft of only a little over a foot. Riverboats are designed not to push through the water but to glide over it and a shallow draft is important," Annabelle said.

"You really know about the boats, don't you?" Fargo said.

"Daddy taught me. He was the one with all the new innovations. Pine will be the wood of the future for all riverboats," Annabelle said as she continued to take him on a tour of the vessel. As night fell the lights went on to make the boat a magical, glowing island. Annabelle's tour took in the upper decks, the dining salon, the gaming room and some of the staterooms, finally halting at one near the stern of the center deck. She opened the door and led him into a room where a small lamp illuminated a bed, chair, and a small dresser. "This is your room for the night," she said.

Fargo lowered himself onto the edge of the bed, found it comfortable and a smile edged his lips as he met Annabelle's waiting gaze. "Just what am I supposed to troubleshoot?" he asked.

"Nothing, tonight. On a regular basis you'd be expected to keep your eyes out for any kind of trouble. A boat can pick up trouble at any port, card sharks, confidence men, plain holdup artists. Then there are occasional Indian attacks. I want someone like you who could handle anything that comes along. You'd change boats often. Word will get out that you could show up anywhere. Troublesome characters will get the message and go to other lines," Annabelle said.

"You've got things pretty well laid out," Fargo said.

"I haven't mentioned the best part," she said.

"Which is?" Fargo frowned.

Her hand went to the buttons at the top of the one-piece outfit, pulled them open with one quick motion and the longish, creamy breasts seemed to spring free from the garment and she was against him, pushing him back onto the bed, one breast finding his mouth, the flat little tip brushing back and forth across his lips. "Your bonus," Annabelle murmured and in what seemed split seconds he was holding her nakedness against his. The riverboat rolled gently at its mooring and the scent of jasmine wafted in from the night and Annabelle's long legs and tiny, flat nipples completed the transformation to another world. She was everything she had been the night before and more, her tight, focused energy again surging, the flat little v rubbing against his groin, her moist portal welcoming, embracing, her body transmitting ecstasy and passion that made his all the more consuming.

The sounds of pure pleasure echoed twice as the night deepened before she lay beside him, all warm rubbing and sweet sensation until finally she lay breathing softly, one longish breast against his mouth until she finally rose onto one elbow, a Cheshire cat smile on her lips as she looked down at him. "Tell me this won't be much more enjoyable than bothering about what happened to Judy Simmons's pa?" she asked.

"No question about that," Fargo agreed. "You telling me you're going to be a steady part of my working for you?"

"Absolutely," Annabelle said, sitting up and reaching for the dark blue garment. "Sleep on it and we'll talk tomorrow," she said.

"You're not staying?" Fargo frowned.

"I want to be home when Barton returns with Garret. It's important I be there. It'll make Garret realize that I'm being harsh on him for his own good," Annabelle said, donning the garment and stepping to the door. "You've never had to be concerned with someone such as Garret so you can't understand what it takes to do it."

"Guess not," Fargo said as Annabelle reached the door. "What'll happen if he refuses to listen to you some time?" he asked.

Annabelle's small smile was slightly chiding. "That won't happen," she said.

"Maybe it's happening and you just don't know it," Fargo said and she frowned back at him. "Maybe he's asserting himself by going around you," Fargo said.

Her smile returned, tolerance in it now. "That's not happening, either," she said. "Sleep tight." He watched the door close after her and lay back. She was very confident of herself. Or of Garret's weakness. But he'd seen overconfidence topple others. She had said the weak had to constantly try to prove they weren't weak. But the weak devised their own ways to prove that. One way was to let the strong underestimate their deviousness. Fargo swore softly. Annabelle was certain she was in control. But was she? And if that family struggle was taking place, how did it involve Judy's pa and the murders? Maybe it didn't, Fargo pondered. Maybe two parallel factors were taking place that only seemed to touch on each other. Was he indulging in his own wild conjectures, Fargo wondered. He was certain of only one thing. He was damn well going to find out the truth of it. With another soft curse, he closed his eyes and enjoyed the luxury of his surroundings.

He woke with the first of the new day, dressed and went outside where he found a stable to buy feed for the Tobiano as the morning sun flooded the blue of the Mississippi and the riverboat rocking gently at its banks. He watched another large riverboat travel past going upriver and decided to ride along beside it to Flat Corners where he halted at the small wharf. A handful of roustabouts relaxed on the wharf and watched the big boat steam on, plainly uninterested in so small a landing. "Morning," Fargo said to three of the men leaning against a bollard. "You been here all yesterday?"

"Yesterday, last night, this morning," the one said. "Only the small cargo boats stop here, mister."

"I was wondering about the *Molly M.* She was supposed to stop here," Fargo said. "Did she?"

"The *Molly M.?* She's a regular. No, she didn't come by, not yesterday, either," the man said. Fargo felt his lips tighten as a stab of apprehension went through him.

"Thanks," he threw back as he put the horse into a fast canter and headed alongside the Mississippi toward Hannibal, apprehension quickly turning into misgiving.

5

When he reached Hannibal, a major stop on the river, he found some eight riverboats there, half moored to wharves, the others hovering near the shore. It took him a moment to find the *Molly M.* but he did, the last vessel along the wharves at the north end and he spurred the horse forward. He felt a wave of relief go through him as he saw Judy appear and wave to him as he dismounted and hurried to the low port deck. "Got worried when I heard you didn't stop at Flat Corners," he said.

"Unexpected trouble," she said. "Four of the crew were attacked at the saloon, jumped by six men. They're all in the hospital, the mate, my fireman and two deckhands. Two of them may not make it."

"You think it was deliberate?" Fargo asked.

"I don't know," Judy shrugged. "All it did was hold up my sailing until I got a new crew. Couldn't sail without a fireman and a mate. I was lucky, a man came by with fireman's papers and he knew a mate. They're on board now."

"Sounds awful convenient," Fargo said.

"But it's not unusual. Deck hands and others are always coming by looking for work," Judy said and she turned as a man came along the deck, small, wiry in build, with large, bulbous eyes.

"Got enough fire in the boiler to sail, ma'am," he said.

"Good. This is Jack Breyer, the new fireman," Judy said and the man turned his bulbous eyes on Fargo, nodded curtly and Fargo noticed he had small hands. "We'll sail in a few minutes," Judy told him and he hurried away.

"You going to be all right?" Fargo asked her.

"Yes. I can't see that this attack was deliberate. Can't see a reason for it. I've still got the last shipment of borax to deliver. All it did was delay me a day," she said. "Why don't you come along?"

"Can't," Fargo said.

"Annabelle Davison?" Judy asked, a hint of reproach in her tone.

"I told you, I'm going to play along with Annabelle and see if I can't help you at the same time," Fargo said.

"You don't think she's involved in anything," Judy said truculently.

"That's right, but others around her may be. Just be patient," Fargo said and she reached out, her hand touching his cheek.

"I'm sorry. I've no right. You've helped me so much already. You've a right to think whatever you want," Judy said.

"Thanks," Fargo said dryly and she leaned against him and he again felt the surprising softness of her compact body.

"Why don't you meet me in Memphis when we unload Star Shipping's borax?" she suggested.

"Good idea. I'd like a look in that warehouse shed of theirs," Fargo said.

"I told you it was empty when I had a look, except for some lengths of wood in the back," Judy said.

"Maybe it won't be this time. Where can I catch up to you?" Fargo asked.

"I'll stop at St. Louis to pick up firewood, then Chester, Cape Girardeau, Osceloa, and then Memphis," she said as Jack Breyer struck his head around a corner of the foredeck. His hands held a piece of firewood and Fargo saw they were barely able to close around the wood.

"Boiler's hot, m'am," he called.

"We'll cast off," Judy said and the new fireman left as she touched her lips to Fargo's cheek, a fleeting gesture. Then she was hurrying down the deck, a compact form full of energy. Fargo stepped ashore, climbed onto the Tobiano and rode away, heading the horse south. He stopped at Doc Sawyer's place and had a chance to carefully examine the Ovaro. The heavy bandages had been removed and he was heartened at the progress the horse was making, the swelling almost gone. He took the time to give his four-legged friend a good currying and when he finished he went his way. Dark had settled over the land and lamplights were on when he reached the manor house.

He dismounted, started toward the imposing entrance when he heard Annabelle's voice raised in anger. He paused, stepped to one side and glanced through the nearest tall window. She was facing Garret, who wore an expression of defiance and Fargo saw the resentment in his weak face, his lips twitching. "You disobeyed me. I told you to stay away from New Orleans," he heard Annabelle say. "All you want to do is gamble away another fortune."

"I can win," Garret muttered.

"No, you can't. You can't gamble. You've no feel

for cards or dice. You're a born loser. Good God, you've proved that. Look at all the trouble you've caused with your gambling," Annabelle said.

"It's being handled," Garret grumbled.

"At what price, Garret, at what price? No more, Garret. You stay out of New Orleans. No more gambling. I don't want to discuss it again," Annabelle insisted.

"One of these days you're going to stop giving me orders," Garret said.

"One of these days," Annabelle echoed. "Now, go do whatever it is you have to do and forget about gambling."

Fargo stepped back into the dark shadows of the night as he heard Garret move and he watched Annabelle's brother stride from the house and cross to the stables and ranch hand quarters. He waited a moment and then stepped to the doorway and rapped against the door frame. Annabelle turned at once, her frown changing to an instant smile.

"You're back," she said and Fargo took in her tall loveliness. She had lied to him about why Garret had wanted to go to New Orleans. It hadn't been to prove himself following a fight. But he felt only sympathy for her. She'd lied because she was ashamed to tell him the truth, ashamed to tell him her brother was a compulsive gambler. She'd admitted he was weak but she was unwilling to admit he was an irresponsible wastrel and Fargo understood that. It was sisterly love and protectiveness and when she came into his arms he held her again, wondering how many things were going on around her she knew nothing about. "You enjoy yourself on the boat?" Annabelle asked. He nodded and her lips found his for a long, lingering exchange. "Sail on her, or any of our boats. Help me. I need someone like you," she said, her voice soft.

"For a while," he said. "Trial run, you could call it."

"I call it wonderful," she said and linked her arm in his as she led him down the wide corridor to her room. "Garret's angry with me. He'll hang out with Barton until later," she said, slipping off her clothes with easy grace. She pulled him down onto the big four-poster and her body was around his instantly and she made love with a new intensity until finally the room rang with her cries of utter satisfaction. Her breasts against his face, she slept in the warmth of passion's afterglow until she woke, stretched and sat up. "It's getting late," she murmured.

"You throwing me out?" Fargo smiled.

"Only so you'll want me more next time," she laughed and handed his shirt to him. He slipped it on, swung from the bed and dressed.

"When?" he asked.

"When you come back after your first trip," she said. "The *Moonlight Rose* sails tomorrow, all the way to Natchez, but you can go as far as you like and change to one of our boats going back upriver." She put on a robe and pressed against him when he finished dressing. Her green eyes held a Cheshire cat satisfaction that somehow took away from the unvarnished passion she had given. She was a creature of contradictions, he reflected again as he rode from the manor. And as in need of help as Judy Simmons, despite all her wealth.

He had reached the edge of the Davison property and a line of hawthorn when he looked back and saw the glint of a lamp as the stable door opened and two riders emerged. Fargo halted, moved into the trees and watched the two riders come closer, both with their horses at a full canter. He recognized Garret Davison first, then Barton Spender. He let them pass and swung in behind them, staying far back, letting the sound of their horses guide his way. The two men rode with definite purpose, changing from a canter into a gallop after they passed Benton's Landing and Fargo took a low ridge and drew closer. They followed the shoreline of the river to arrive at Flats Corners where Fargo, back on flat land, slowed as the two men rode into town.

He pulled alongside the few buildings along the east side of the main street and drew to a halt as Garret and Barton Spender reined up at the local inn. Both men left their horses and strode into the inn and Fargo tied the Tobiano in a narrow space between two buildings and hurried to the inn. A long lamp lighted an entranceway where a small, stooped man sat behind a desk with a ledger pad atop it. The clerk lifted a pinched face as Fargo entered. "Two men that just came in here, where'd they go?" he asked.

"Don't know that's your business, mister," the man said.

Fargo leaned forward and closed one hand around the stooped little man's shirt, pulling him halfway to his feet. "You're absolutely right, friend. Now answer me and we'll both be happy," he growled.

The man swallowed hard. "Room five, end of the hallway," he said.

"Very good," Fargo said, letting the man fall back into his chair and hurried down an almost dark hallway on silent footsteps. He halted at the end of the hallway at the closed door of a room, pressed his ear against the door and listened. A frown crept across his brow as he heard only silence, not even the sound of a whispered voice. He waited another thirty seconds, then drew his Colt and closed his left hand around the doorknob. He turned, the pistol raised, and eased the door open a fraction. There was still only silence. Moonlight from a lone window illuminated the room enough for him to see a bed against one wall and a figure lying on it. His eyes went to the window. It was open from the bottom. He was across the room to the side of the bed in two long strides and stared down at the figure of a man on the bed on his back, wearing only undershorts. A bone-handled knife rose up from the middle of his chest, buried to the hilt.

Fargo swore as he leaned down to the figure. The man was dead, his eyes closed. He'd been killed asleep, the knife plunged into him before he had a chance to wake up. Fargo went to the window but knew he'd see no one as he peered out and he turned back into the room. A small kerosene lamp rested on a wooden washbasin and Fargo turned the lamp on in order to examine the dead man. He saw a fairly well-built man with graying hair, in his forties, he guessed, with an even-featured face. The man's clothes were neatly laid out over a straight-backed chair; shirt, trousers, jacket.

Fargo started with the jacket, rummaged through the pockets, found only some bills and change in the outside pockets but he felt his eyes narrow as he drew the small silver badge from the inside jacket pocket. With the badge he found a neatly printed card and felt his lip moving as he read:

This Will Identify

WILLIAM BRANTLY

Federal Agent 20

UNITED STATES OF AMERICA

"I'll be damned," Fargo muttered aloud. Putting the badge and card in his pocket, he decided to leave the room the way his killers had, by the window. He swung long legs over the window sill, landed outside and hurried to the front of the inn where, as he knew they would be, the two horses were gone. He retrieved the Tobiano and turned the horse south, held a steady pace until he reached Benton's Landing just as dawn did.

Tim Olson lived over the jailhouse and Fargo pounded on the door until the sheriff came down wearing only trousers and an undershirt. "Fargo. What in tarnation do you want at this hour?" Tim Olson frowned as Fargo strode into the front office.

"Got something for you," Fargo said and tossed the federal agent's badge and identification card on the desk. The Sheriff stared at the two items with a frown.

"By God. Where'd you get these?" Tim asked.

"From his pocket. He's been murdered," Fargo said and the sheriff stared at him.

"Got a letter from his boss telling me to expect a visit from him," Olson said.

"Garret Davison and Barton Spender put a knife through him when he was asleep," Fargo said.

The sheriff's jaw dropped open. "What? You saw them do it?" Fargo's lips pulled back in a grimace as he told Tim Olson about following the two men. "Then you didn't see them do it," she sheriff said. "You know what that means."

"Go ahead," Fargo scowled.

"It means they could've found him that way and split," the sheriff said.

"Bullshit," Fargo snapped.

"Maybe so but you can't prove different. You didn't see anything."

"I don't need to prove different," Fargo said.

"I do," the sheriff said and Fargo glared back. "Why would Garret Davison be involved in murdering a government agent? Give me a reason. I need a reason. The Davison's own a big riverboat line. They're rolling in money," Olson said.

"I don't think Annabelle Davison's involved in anything shady but Garret Davison's a weak sister. God knows what he'd get into to prove himself a big man. Maybe he wants the kind of money that Annabelle controls," Fargo said. "Hell, you saying you don't believe me?"

"I'm saying you didn't see them do it. You can't give me proof. You can't even give me a reason why Garret Davison would do something like that. I need proof, reasons, connections."

Fargo swore softly as he muttered. "Why would a government agent be coming to see you?"

"The letter said there's a government gold repository in Iowa, near Council Bluffs. Seems they use it to store gold dust. When they get enough of it they ship it back east where it's made into gold bars. But it seems the gold dust has been disappearing and they can't figure how it's being stolen. Agent Brantly was coming here to see if anybody has been selling gold dust. It seems they've two more agents working different parts of the country." Sheriff Olson let out a weary sigh. "Hell, I've heard nothing about anybody peddling gold dust. It's sure as hell not the Davisons."

"Why did Garret Davison and Spender go to Will Brantly?" Fargo asked. "There has to be a reason."

"Find it. Give me something I can run with,"

the sheriff said. "I'll send somebody up to get Will Brantly and notify his boss."

Fargo rose unhappily and went outside where the new sun had begun to flood the day. He rode from the town, along the river and halted beneath a thick cluster of horse chestnut, took down his bedpack and stretched out in the shade. He felt like a man who'd been shadowboxing until exhaustion. This was just another thing that refused to connect, an act that couldn't be given a reason, murder without motive. But it had to tie in somehow. Or did it? He had to again consider the possibility that there was no central connection, that two, or maybe more, disconnected things were going on. But he snorted as he threw aside the thought. The attack on Judy, the deaths of her pa and Captain Thompson, the sinkings of their boats and now the murder of a government agent. The same players kept turning up, Garret Davison and Bart Spendor and the mysterious Star Shipping Company.

There had to be a key that would connect it all. But what? The question continued to dance mockingly in his mind until he turned it off and drew sleep around himself. It was noon when he woke and he decided he'd go to meet Judy in Memphis. Pondering for a moment, he concluded he'd make better time by horse than boat and after saddling the Tobiano he turned the horse south, but he stayed on higher ground away from the river. He had taken a narrow road along a line of bitternut when he saw a lone rider peering down from a ridge above him. The man watched him go by and Fargo stayed on the road and spotted another horseman, on the other side of the road, also quietly sitting his horse. Fargo rode on past the second figure but suddenly felt the hair on the back of his neck grow stiff.

He swore softly. He knew the sign. His sixth sense had been triggered. It was a sign that never steered him wrong. He kept the horse on the road as he glanced back at a curve in the road. The second horseman had disappeared and Fargo's lips tightened. The first horseman had also left, he was certain. A long stand of red ash loomed up some thousand yards ahead, thick and dense, with plenty of underbrush inside it. And something else, Fargo noted. He steered the horse left to the leading edge of the forest. They'd be back inside a ways, waiting for him to pass by or ride through. He wouldn't want to disappoint them, Fargo thought as he slid from the horse.

Walking on steps silent as a cougar's tread, he led the horse into the forest, staying in a half-crouch beside the animal's side. He drew the big Henry from its saddlecase as he dropped to the ground, gave the Tobiano a sharp pat on the rump and watched the horse move forward. Fargo crouched beside the trunk of a thick ash and watched the horse slow and then walk on through the trees. He dropped to his stomach on a bed of elf cap moss, and inched forward, his eyes scanning the forest in front of him. Suddenly he stopped, a sound reaching him, that of a hoof coming down slowly, almost silently, then another and still another.

He waited and the horsemen appeared, threading their way through the trees. They rode with space between them. He counted six. They moved their horses slowly as they peered into the forest and suddenly he saw them spot the Tobiano. Three of them shifted direction and went after the piebald horse at once while the other three held back. "Shit," he heard one of the first three bite out. They had reached the Tobiano and found the horse riderless. Fargo lifted the big Henry and fired two shots in fast succession. Two of the three horsemen nearest him jerked in their saddles and toppled from their horses as though they were part of a synchronized maneuver.

The third rider dove from his horse as Fargo's shot grazed his back. He hit the ground, rolled and fired two shots in the general direction of where Fargo lay on the ground. But Fargo had rolled, coming up against another tree trunk. With a quick glance to his right, he glimpsed the other three riders moving toward him. He fired again, the rifle a heavy sound in the thickness of the forest. One of the three men emitted a gargling sound as he toppled forward, clung for a moment to his horse's mane and then slid to the ground. Fargo glimpsed the figure running toward him, saw the man holding two six-guns.

Diving, Fargo hit the ground, rolled into a patch of five-foot tall pokeweed as a hail of bullets hurtled past him. The rifle felt suddenly awkward, so he dropped the Henry and drew his Colt, rolled again in the pokeweed and felt another shot whistle past his shoulder. The shooter continued to charge as he fired both guns and, lying on his stomach, Fargo fired a single shot that caught the man full in his abdomen. With a groaned cough, the man stumbled forward and collapsed at the edge of the cluster of weeds. Fargo lay still, listening. There were two more left and he hardly breathed. They were hired drygulchers, not hunters. They had neither the temperament nor the training to stalk their quarry. He had only to wait. He counted off less than a minute when he heard the sound from his left, that of one of the men moving through the forest with what he thought was stealth.

But the man's foot pressed onto a dry leaf and his body brushed against the edge of the pokeweed, his other foot sliding along the grass, making a soughing sound that Fargo's ears picked up. He waited another moment and his finger was on the trigger of the Colt when the man came into view. He fired and the figure disappeared with a hollow groan. Fargo didn't move. The silence suddenly erupted with the sound of twigs being shoved aside and running footsteps. The sixth drygulcher was running to his horse and Fargo rose on one knee, his eyes sweeping the trees as his ears focused on the sound of the fleeing figure. He dropped the Colt into its holster and scooped up the big Henry as he spotted the man with one foot in the stirrup of his horse.

"Hold it right there and you stay alive," Fargo called. The man ignored his order and pulled himself into the saddle. He never got a chance to dig his heels into the side of the horse. The rifle barked. The man seemed to shiver in the saddle before he toppled backwards from the horse and lay still on the ground. Fargo rose and walked to where his attackers lay strewn in a half-circle. He stared down at them for a moment. Ordinary hired gunmen, he saw, and knew that searching them would tell him nothing. Besides, he already knew one answer and he walked away, found the Tobiano pulling young leaves from the low branches, and climbed onto the horse. He rode form the forest not with anger but cloaked instead with a terrible sadness. He couldn't go on without returning to Benton's Landing. Tim Olson would want to know what had happened.

The sun had crossed into the afternoon when

he reached the town and drew up before the sheriff's office. Tim Olson looked up from his desk as Fargo entered, surprise digging into his face. "Fargo," he said with a frown, "didn't expect you back so soon."

The sadness inside him stayed in Fargo's slow smile. "I know. You didn't expect me back at all," he said.

The sheriff's frown deepened. "What's that mean?"

"It means six bastards were watching for me and tried to kill me," Fargo said.

"You saying Garret Davison and Spender again?" the sheriff asked.

"Not directly. They didn't know I saw them go into Will Brantly's room. They didn't know I discovered they'd murdered him. They went out the window so the desk clerk wouldn't see them leave. Only one person knew and that's because I told him," Fargo said and watched the sheriff's eyes cloud over. "How long have you been in Garret Davison's pocket, old friend?" Fargo asked.

The sheriff's shoulders lifted in a small, apologetic shrug. "Long enough," he said, blowing a deep sigh from his lips. "Little things, at first, then bigger stuff. This lousy job never paid much."

"So Davison paid you enough to buy your soul," Fargo said, the sadness still clinging. "How do you live with yourself, old friend? How do you look in the mirror?" He saw Tim Olson's eyes look away, then return, a strange kind of pain inside them. "How many others have you betrayed? How many others who trusted you have you had killed?"

"Does it matter?" the man returned, bitterness flooding his face.

"It matters, most of all to you," Fargo said.

"You think you're telling me something I don't

know," Olson shot back with a sudden burst of savagery. "It's hard the first time, then it gets easier."

"And you keep on," Fargo said.

"Why not? There's no going back. There's no undoing what's done," Olson said.

"I'm sorry for you, old friend, almost as sorry as you are for yourself," Fargo said and the sheriff stared back with bitterness in his eyes. "But you tried to have me killed. I'm going to take you in, to Hannibal. There's a sheriff there. You can tell me what this is all about on the way."

"I've got money. You can have it," Olson said.

"You know better," Fargo returned. He saw Tim Olson's hand start to move toward the Remington in his holster. "Don't," he said. "You know better than to try to outdraw me."

The man's hand halted and he slowly nodded. "Yes, I know," he said, waited a moment and then his hand shot downward and yanked at the gun. Fargo's answer was automatic, his draw lightning fast, the big Colt clearing the holster and firing in one flashing motion. Sheriff Tim Olson knocked over the chair behind him as he flew backwards, his chest erupting in a spray of red. He hit the wall and slid downwards, lifeless before he reached the floor.

Fargo stared down at him. "Goddammit, you knew, you knew," he murmured and the terrible realization flooded through him. Olson had indeed known what his action would trigger. In an agonizing moment he had chosen. In an inner explosion of guilt, he had elected to pay. Fargo turned away as he wondered how long it had taken this moment to arrive and realized the answer was one no man would ever know.

Outside, he climbed onto the Tobiano and

turned the horse south. He'd not go to find Garret Davison, not yet. He'd only hear more denials there and he still had no proof. He needed that final key before he faced Garret Davison with the truth. And brought pain to Annabelle.

6

He rode at a steady pace, the Mississippi in sight as it generally wound and curved its way in the same direction. Night fell and he swore at the delays that had slowed him. In the distance, he could see the glow of the big side-wheelers that became little moving islands of light. He halted a little before midnight, bedded down alongside a cluster of bitternut and slept until the new day dawned. He rode again, pausing only to let the horse drink from a pond. He finally passed Cairo and realizing how far he still had to go, increased his pace.

Another night descended and he chafed at having to stop but he knew the full day's hard ride had taken its toll on the Tobiano as well as himself. He bedded down and was again in the saddle soon after the pink of dawn touched the sky. He reached a spot some dozen miles above Memphis when he crossed to the east bank of the river over a shallow sandbar that only required the horse swim a few hundred yards. He reached Memphis and saw the crowded, busy waterfront with a line of riverboats tied at the wharves. He searched for the *Molly M.* but didn't see her, though he saw three large side-wheelers that carried the Davison Line pennant.

He rode up to a small wooden shack that sat at the base of the center wharf, the word DOCKMASTER painted across the front of it. Dismounting, he entered the shack and found a man wearing a skipper's cap and a pair of suspenders over an undershirt, which held up baggy trousers. Ruddy-complexioned and gray-bearded, the man looked up at once, experienced eyes taking in his visitor instantly. "Good day, stranger. Now, what brings you here?" the man asked. "Something different, I'm sure."

"What makes you say that?" Fargo asked.

The dockmaster's shrewd eyes crinkled. "Because I can spot a riverboat drifter looking for a berth, a freight hauler with a bill of lading, a gaming man looking to know what boat's got a gambling parlor and just about any other type comes by regularly," he said.

"Fair enough," Fargo smiled. "First, I was looking for a riverboat, the *Molly M.*"

"Cap Walker's boat. I was surprised to see Judy Simmons aboard as skipper," he said. "She explained why to me."

"Then she's here?" Fargo asked.

"Was here, came in yesterday, left this morning," the dockmaster said. "A haulage outfit came, picked up her cargo and she left. She said someone might come looking for her. I guess that'd be you?"

"Got delayed," Fargo said. "While I'm here, I'd like the logbooks of the *Judy Belle* and Captain Thompson's boat."

"Can't give them to you but I can let you look at them," the man said. He rose and sorted through a shelf behind him. Pulling out two logbooks, he handed them to Fargo. "Sit down over there," he said, gesturing to a swivel chair in a corner of the room beside a window that let him look out over the river and the collection of vessels.

"Much obliged," Fargo said and took the two logbooks into the corner. He began to examine each of them as a parade of visitors came by to see the dockmaster, among them riverboat skippers, freight haulers with bills of lading, and cargo owners protesting unloading delays. Fargo blotted out the distractions and concentrated on the logbooks, taking the *Judy Belle*'s first. He went through pages of cargo listings, docking times, and notations of weather conditions and navigation problems. The cargo listings for Star Shipping began late in the book and seemed ordinary enough except for the volume which all but eliminated any other cargo. When he finished the last page he took up Captain Thompson's log. He found much the same kind of notations and Star Shipping also took over all the vessel's cargo space when they began shipments.

Fargo grimaced when he finished. There'd been nothing unusual in either log but he went over the *Judy Belle*'s book again. He was frowning when he finished this time and quickly opened the other boat's log. His frown dug deeper. There had been no shipments from Star Shipping aboard when the *Judy Belle* sank. None aboard Captain Thompson's boat, either. He rifled through the pages of both books as he felt the grim excitement pushing through him. The *Judy Belle* had unloaded her last Star Shipping cargo, the seventh shipment, when she was sunk and Judy's pa killed. The other boat had just delivered her twelfth shipment before she and her captain went down. More than a coincidence, Fargo muttered as he stared at the pages and he leaped to his feet, a thought exploding in his mind. Judy had just delivered a shipment last night.

He thrust the logbooks at the dockmaster. "The *Molly M.* went upriver. You know where she'd be making her first stop?" he asked.

"Judy told me she'd lay over at Cairo to take on supplies," the man said. "I'd guess she'd be there a little before dark."

Fargo raced from the hut and leaped onto the Tobiano, sent the horse down the crowded waterfront streets and turned inland. He rode north, not bothering to parallel the river's twisting course as he raced in the straightest line he could find. He detoured to skirt a series of sharp rises, edged closer to the river and then away again as he found an unused wagon train path, the wide Conestoga wheel tracks still pressed into the ground. He pushed the horse as hard as he dared and wished he was on his Ovaro with its powerful, ground-eating stride and phenomenal endurance. But the sun moved inexorably across the sky and time refused to slow its pace and he heard himself cursing as the day slid toward its end. He made three stops to let the horse rest its tired muscles and to avoid the danger of foundering and felt the animal's exhaustion as he passed Reelfoot and Hickman.

But Cairo lay directly ahead and the day still clung as he pressed the horse forward. When he cut to the river and rounded the bend, Cairo spread out before him and he slowed as he saw the dozens and dozens of riverboats moored next to each other, waiting their turn at the relatively few wharves. He rode along the river edge, his eyes peering at the steamers, some side-wheelers, some stern-wheelers, reading off names: *Bonnie*

Mary, Accord, Queenie, Paducah City, Jennie Bell, Dauntless, Southern Star, Delta Lady in what seemed an unending procession of them. They were moored side by side, many with but a few feet of river between them. He counted at least five with the Davison line pennant as he searched for the *Molly M.* Most of the vessels were the large passenger boats with their double iron chimneys rising high with the smaller cargo boats crowding closer to the shore.

Blending together as they did, hard upon each other, they tended to look alike and he frowned as he searched to find the *Molly M.* But he found her suddenly and reined to a halt. She was almost hidden between two large paddle wheelers, and a good five hundred yards from the shore. He dismounted and led the horse back from the wharves and tied the animal beneath a pair of big sandbar willows. A quick glance at the sky told him the dusk was beginning to roll forward and he hurried to the nearest wharf where a half-dozen roustabouts lounged. "Want to get to a boat in midriver," Fargo said. "Do I have to swim?"

"We can raft you over," one of the men said. "Fifty cents."

"Let's go," Fargo said and two of the men rose and led him to the side of the wharf where a small wooden raft was tied, hardly more than a handful of logs strapped together. He climbed onto it with one of the men while the other untied the single mooring line. Using a long pole with a flattened side on one end, the roustabout sent the raft into the river. Guiding the square raft with expert skill, he moved past three of the larger riverboats, followed where Fargo pointed, and drew up alongside the *Molly M.* Fargo tossed him a fifty-cent coin and climbed aboard the boat. He was struck

103

first by the silence. There seemed no one on board. Moving along the low, narrow deck, he made for the captain's cabin, grateful for the slowness of the dusk, reached it and found the door closed.

He knocked, heard a sound from inside and then Judy opened the door. The surprise on her round face instantly changed to delight and her arms flew around his neck as she hugged him to her. "I was worried. You didn't show at Memphis," she said and then stepped back and looked apologetic. "Sorry," she said.

"I'm not," he told her and stepped into the small cabin with one cot against the wall. "Had some delays getting to you," he said as he closed the door of the cabin. He told her first about the murder of the government agent, then the attack on him, and finally he told her about Tim Olson.

She stared back with shock and surprise in her face. "My God," she said. "He was friendly with the Davisons but I'd never have expected this. "But what's it all mean? How does it fit together? It's plain the Davisons are part of it but part of what?"

"Garret Davison," Fargo corrected.

"Your opinion," she sniffed.

"You're letting jealousy get in the way of logic," he said and she let her little pug nose crinkle. "But I'm thinking that Star Shipping is involved, somehow, someway. I think we ought to go back and have another look at that warehouse of theirs in Memphis."

"Why didn't you look at it while you were there?" Judy asked.

"I was figuring to but I came onto something that sent me racing up to find you," he said and told her about the discovery he'd made in the log-books.

She paled for a moment as his words sank into her and then her arms were around his neck again. This time her mouth found his, stayed, soft sweetness, pressing until she drew back a fraction. "You're damn wonderful," she murmured. "Thank you, thank you." She pressed her lips to his again when he felt the sudden shudder, too strong to be her. It came again, instantly, then again and Judy drew back. The entire boat was shuddering, each tremor more violent than the one before until suddenly there was only a continuous shuddering. Judy flung the door open and raced out. "That's got to be the boiler," she said.

He raced down the deck after her toward the stern. The boat was shuddering violently, planks rubbing against one another. "Jack!" she called out. "Jack Breyer!" But there was no answer from the new fireman and Fargo was at her side when she reached the boiler. Tendrils of steam were rising from the boiler and he saw the firebox jammed full and blazing. "The water injection's been shut off, the safety valves locked down," Judy gasped. "Everything's too hot to touch."

The boat gave a tremendous shudder more violent than any of the others. Fargo grabbed Judy around the waist and yanked her to the edge of the deck. "She's about to blow," he shouted as he dove into the water, holding onto her. They hit the water together, sank and then swam up. His head just broke the surface, Judy beside him, when the *Molly M.* exploded in a tremendous, earsplitting sound. The entire vessel came apart in a flying collection of decks, cabins, planks, and pilot house. He saw the boiler sail into the air in a parabolic arc and land in the center of a riverboat moored fifty feet away. The stern paddle disintegrated as though it were suddenly a giant collection of matchsticks, only the matchsticks weighed tens of pounds and were driven by thousands of pounds of force. "Down," Fargo said as wood rained down all around them and he pulled her underwater with him, held there until his breath gave out and surfaced, pulling Judy with him.

The scene had turned into something from hell. The explosion and fire had come down on other vessels, which instantly caught fire. Some also exploded and in turn they rained down burning fireballs on more vessels. In what seemed like only seconds, Fargo guessed there were at least twenty boats blazing, flames running like wildfire from boat to boat moored alongside each other, consuming the light wood as if it were so much kindling. He saw bodies flying into the air, some cut in half. An iron funnel toppled and he saw it decapitate at least six people. Others were on fire, clothes soaked in burning kerosene and oil, some leaping into the water to try and save themselves.

"Swim to shore, underwater as much as you can," he yelled at Judy.

She pulled at his arm. "What are you going to do?" she asked.

"Try to save some of those people," he said. "Now, swim, dammit!" He pushed her head down and saw her form move off underwater and then he turned and struck out for the middle of the river. He had to veer from one side to the other, dive under the surface at other times, as the water now burned with patches of oil and kerosene. Spotting a bobbing head, he reached out and caught hold of a man who had all but exhausted his ability to breathe. "Relax," he said. "I've got you." He swam with the man until they were close enough to the shore for others to rush out and take him. Returning to the river, Fargo swam out again, spotted two children clinging to a piece of wood and got them ashore. Dusk had probably descended, he realized, but the scene was bright as day with the light of the burning riverboats. He swam forward, around a circle of water ablaze with oil, came upon an elderly women barely clinging to a floating door as a riverboat began to go under perilously close to her.

He reached her, held her onto the door and steered everyone to shore where others waded out and took charge. He turned to see some of the riverboat skippers had gotten up enough steam to turn their paddle wheels and they sailed away from the scene of blazing boats and pitiful cries. But there were only a few capable of escaping, Fargo saw, most of the boats sinking in fiery pyres, hissing as they went under, crying out as though they were flesh and blood. Small boats and rafts had put out from the shore, little knots of rescuers coming to the aid of those they could still help.

Fargo struck out for the wharves, pieces of which had holes in their planking, others burning from lengths of wood that had crashed onto them like burning spears. He found a spot and pulled himself from the river, lay still for a moment and drew in deep draughts of air. He raised his head when he heard his name being called and saw Judy running toward him. "I pretty much didn't take my eyes off you," she said, sinking down beside him. She was still soaking wet, her blue shirt clinging to her as a leaf clings to a wet rock, high, round breasts outlined, little points pressing into the fabric. She leaned against him and her voice trembled. "Oh, God, it all started on the *Molly M.*," she said.

"No fault of yours," he told her.

"Depends on how you look at it," she said. "It was deliberate, the boiler put on full, all the safety valves turned off. I was in my cabin the past two hours. It had to be Jack Breyer."

"Your new fireman," Fargo grunted. "Only he was never a riverboat fireman. His hands were too small. I should've paid more attention to that."

"The attack on the regular crew was no simple barroom brawl. It was done so I'd need new crewmen. He happened by, a stroke of luck, I thought. Some luck," Judy bit out.

"It was to be one more accident. They'd see that the boat blew up and you'd have been killed and there'd be nobody to say it wasn't an accident. Once more, after delivery of the last shipment," Fargo said. She shivered but it wasn't just because of the terrible truth that had swept over her. He pulled her to her feet with him. "Let's get those wet clothes off you," he said and led her from the wharves back to the sandbar willows where he'd left the Tobiano. He took a blanket from his saddlebag and gave it to her. Stepping into the thickness of the drooping willow leaves, she shed her clothes and emerged with the blanket wrapped around her. He had taken off everything but trousers and swung her into the saddle in front of him.

"There's a cabin, about a half-mile straight west," Judy said. "Pa bought it some years ago. He wanted a place to get away from the river but not too far away."

"Sounds perfect," Fargo said and set the horse west on a narrow path. The night had come, he saw as he rode from the still fire-tinged sky around the riverfront and Judy supplied directions until the small cabin came into view. The night

had stayed warm and she entered first as he unsaddled the horse. She had put on a small fire
when he entered the cabin but still sat with the
blanket wrapped around her. He spread out her
wet clothes and his shed trousers and laid them
out to dry by the fire. Wearing only undershorts,
he sat down on a thick bearskin rug and saw
Judy's eyes take in the muscled beauty of his body.
"We pay a visit tomorrow," he said, "to the Star
Shipping warehouse. Maybe there's something
there that'll give us a lead."

"It was empty when I visited it, except for some
pieces of wood against the back wall," Judy said.
"Maybe we'll have better luck this time." She rose,
came down to sit beside him. "But that's tomorrow. I don't want to think about what's going to
happen and I don't want to think about what just
happened. I know I wouldn't be here if you hadn't
come for me, if you hadn't picked up what the logbooks said. I just want now and you and to forget
the rest of the world."

Judy shrugged her shoulders and the blanket
dropped from her and she knelt naked in front of
him, a faintly rosy hue to her skin, the firm, compact body somehow radiating energy even when
quiet. He took in breasts that were very round and
firm, standing out with a kind of physical pride to
them that seemed to echo the aggressiveness of
her little pug nose. Small, very dark pink nipples
were already standing against small, dark pink circles. Beneath the round breasts, a barrel-chested
rib cage added to the compactness of her. A
slightly convex little belly fitted perfectly between
solid, wide hips and a bushy triangle of curly
blackness. Youth and firm flesh kept her legs from
chunkiness, adding instead a kind of energetic
beauty that reached out with its own sensuous-

ness. She leaned forward, arms encircling him and he felt the softness of her breasts press into his chest and then she was atop him on the rug, mouth pressing his lips, all wanting eagerness.

He answered, felt her tongue dart out, touch, draw back, dart again, surrogate gestures and suddenly Judy was a charged package of softness, the compact little body astride him, rubbing, moving from side to side, the fleshy little belly against his groin. He felt himself responding, growing and hardening against her belly. "Oh, God, oh, yes, yes," she cried out and then she was rubbing the bushy, black triangle over him, exchanging sensations, compact yet soft flesh alive with its own energy. She pressed one round breast into his mouth and he took it, let his lips, then his tongue, caress the small tip until it strained against its delicate flesh. He rolled then, taking her with him, holding his muscled body to her and Judy gasped out little sounds of pleasure, words of the body, sighs as soft yet as demanding as the touch of her breasts.

He slid his hand downwards, through the bushy blackness, down further to the firm thighs and she was warm and he pressed further and felt the sweet stickiness of her as she closed her thighs around his hand. She clasped him there for a long moment, then let her legs fall away and he pushed upwards to the tip of the quivering, waiting lips. "Jeeeesus, oh, Jeeeesus," Judy gasped out and her heels dug into the rug and her torso lifted, almost leaping upwards. "Oh, come in, come in, oh, please, oh Jesus, please," she cried out and again her body leaped upwards. He slid fingers forward and touched the lubricious invitation and her chunky thighs rose to clasp against him. Her hands were digging into his buttocks, pulling at him, frantic wanting in their strength and he brought his maleness up, let himself enter, slowly exploring, then faster and Judy's body stiffened, relaxed, flung itself upwards. "Ah, ah, aaaaah," she breathed and she rose with him, pushed against his every slow thrust, suddenly exploding with a frantic bucking and bulling, the hunger of her consuming and enveloping, all the compact energy of her exploding in a frenzy of ecstacy.

She cried out, half-laughed, half-screamed as she bucked and thrust herself upwards with him and he felt himself carried along with her energetic frenzy, the unbridled passion of her that refused all subtlety, rejecting all languor. Very round breasts bouncing against him with her every leaping thrust, Judy rushed the final moment with complete and utter concentration, the senses following the flesh, ecstasy pursuing energy and suddenly he felt her arms stiffen around him. For a second, her bucking, leaping, twisting compact body froze in midair, to continue with renewed, shuddering frenzy.

"Now, now, now, oh Jeeeeezus, now, yes, yes, now," Judy screamed and he felt her contractions seizing him and he was carried with her, joining her rapture, the fusion of burning moments, explosion of the senses, that instant of absolute union yet absolute aloneness. Judy made little sounds of protest as the ecstacy spiraled into that memory never fully recaptured and she clung to him with her body still making tiny motions, the flesh unwilling to capitulate to the evanescence of the senses. Finally she lay still beside him but she kept her bushy black triangle pressed hard against him and he smiled at the little gesture of refusal.

"Relax, honey," he said gently. "We can do it again."

"We better," she said, the hint of a pout in her

voice. She pushed herself up on one elbow, the very round breasts beautifully firm as the tiny tips brushed against his chest. "I don't want a passing night with you."

"No passing night," he said and cupped one firm breast in his hand. "How about a passing month?"

"That'd be better," she said. "Two would be still better."

"We'll see," he said. "Now, I think we could use some sleep. Tomorrow could be a busy day." She nodded, settled herself down beside him and he heard her steady breathing in moments. He closed his eyes and thought of the fiery carnage at the riverfront and was certain of one thing. Finding the key that connected it all together would not be enough. The guilty would not sit back. Their hands were too bloody. He'd have to bring them down before they came after him again. He could do no less. He turned on his side and slept wrapped in grimness.

When morning came, he woke and found their clothes had dried and he was almost dressed when Judy sat up. He watched her as she rose, washed from a small basin in a corner of the cabin and began to dress. Once again, he was taken by how her compact body exuded its own brand of sensuousness. She was her own contradiction that worked and she waited until she had fully dressed before she came to him, pressed her mouth on his. "I know you want to get moving. I didn't want to make it too hard for you," she said and followed the remark with a giggle.

"We're going to have to stop back at Cairo," Fargo said. "I don't know what we'll run into. I don't want the two of us on one horse."

"There's a man runs a stable a few streets down

from the center of town. He used to ship horses with us from time to time," Judy said. He nodded and helped her onto the Tobiano when he'd finished saddling the horse and swung on behind her. Her full little rear pressed against him as they rode, a reminder of how it had bucked and leaped only a few hours before. She rode in silence and he watched her face grow stiff as they reached the riverfront. She took quick glances at the charred hulks that remained afloat, only a few hadn't been entirely consumed. He threaded a path through the crowds of concerned and curious that lined the riverfront streets and Judy directed him to the stable.

He found a horse for her there, a nice, tan filly with a good spring of rib and after pausing to breakfast at a tavern nearby he rode south from Cairo, staying near the river. "Been thinking about something," Fargo said as Judy rode beside him and he set a steady pace. "You had the flash about Captain Sam being in trouble, that sixth sense. It was so strong you had to go to him and you were right. I was impressed, until last night." Judy shot a questioning look at him. "How come you didn't have any sense they were getting ready to blow the boat up under you?"

"You think the thing with Captain Sam was a lucky coincidence?" Judy said.

"It makes me wonder," he admitted.

"No coincidence. I get flashes like that often, and I'm always right. But only concerning other people. I never get any flashes about myself," she said.

"Work on it," he said. "It'd sure come in handy." She shrugged and fell silent and rode beside him as he increased the pace. When they reached Memphis there was still light left in the day and

Judy remembered her way down a long street of warehouses that stretched back from the river-front wharves. She slowed as they neared the end of the street and she pointed to a warehouse standing alone, the last one on the street. Fargo pulled the horses behind a larger shed a dozen yards away and dismounted. "Stay here," he said, drawing the Colt. "I want to check it out myself first." She nodded but he saw her press herself against a corner of the building where she could watch him as he started toward the warehouse.

He moved in a crouch to the back of the shed before making his way to the wide door in the front. Pressed against the door, he listened for sounds from inside and heard only silence. He stayed, his ears straining, but he continued to hear neither voices nor movement. He carefully pulled the wide door open, stayed in his crouch, the Colt ready to fire, but saw that the warehouse was empty. He straightened, motioned to Judy who ran over and stepped inside with him. "Nothing, no barrels, nothing, same as when I stopped here," she said.

"But they were here," Fargo said, bending down to the floor and pointing out the residue of white borax powder.

"But nothing else, except those pieces of wood at the back I mentioned to you," Judy said and Fargo strode across the warehouse.

"Let's have a look at them," he said and she followed to stand beside him. She saw a furrow crossing his brow. "These aren't just pieces of wood," he said, lifting one of them. "This is a Long Tom," he said and took up another. "This is a sluice, and here's a riffle box and a cradle."

"What are they?"

"These are all devices for separating gold.

They're used by miners to separate gold dust or flakes from dirt and gravel. Only these were used to separate the gold dust from the borax," Fargo said and Judy's eyes grew wide.

"The gold dust stolen from the government repository. It was shipped in the borax barrels," she said.

"And then separated here," Fargo said.

"Garret Davison?"

"With Barton Spender as his right-hand man."

"Why?" Judy frowned. "He's got plenty of money. He owns the biggest riverboat fleet on the Mississippi."

"Annabelle has the money. She controls the business. This is his way of getting rich himself," Fargo said. "Star Shipping's a dummy company he set up as a front."

"But why didn't he ship the borax on his own boats? It would've been easier and simpler. Why did he use Pa's boat and the others? And why did he kill Pa and Captain Thompson and try to kill Sam Walker and me? Why did he have to sink everyone's boat?"

Fargo's face wrinkled as he frowned into space. "I can't figure that but there has to be a reason. It was all very cleverly figured out, all carefully planned, every trail covered, every murder and every sinking made to seem an accident, just in case someone beside Tim Olson should investigate," Fargo said.

"Such as who? I was the only one who gave a damn. I was the only one who never believed the story about Pa's death," Judy said.

"Yes, but there were government agents trying to track down the stolen gold dust. He knew that. There was always the chance an agent would ask too many questions," Fargo said.

"It would still have been simpler to ship on their own boats. They wouldn't have had to cover up any of the killings, which still don't make sense. Something doesn't fit about that."

"You're right. That's one of the questions we still need to get answered," Fargo said and walked out of the warehouse. "Meanwhile, let's see if we can find out where they've taken the gold dust," he said and pointed to the two sets of wagon tracks.

"It's almost dark," Judy said.

"We can follow. With a wagon they'll stick to roads," Fargo said and climbed onto his horse. With Judy alongside, he trailed the tracks of the two wagons as they led southward down a wide road that grew narrower as the night deepened. He stayed with the trail until the road grew thick with grass and then found a spot to bed down in a stand of hackberry. Judy slept quickly in his arms, too tired for anything more, and when morning came he found a stream with which to wash and a cluster of wild plums for breakfast. In the daylight, the wagon tracks were visible again in the grass and he followed as the road turned and led away from the river, curved inland to cut through forest and low hills. He turned from the road into the trees but kept within sight of the path and they had gone almost to mid-afternoon when he held up his hand and reined to a halt.

Judy followed his gaze and saw the two wagons pulled to one side of the road, six figures lounging beside them. Fargo dismounted and she stayed at his heels as he moved closer on foot. He heard her gasped whisper as she saw the man leaning against the first wagon. "Jack Breyer," she whispered and Fargo motioned to the six canvas sacks in the wagons.

"The gold dust," he said. "They got rid of the barrels and the borax after separating it."

"Why'd they stop?" Judy asked.

"They're waiting for somebody," Fargo said and moved closer after draping the horse's reins over a low branch. He sank to one knee when they were some two dozen yards away and as close as he dared go. His ears caught the sound of approaching hoofbeats before Jack Breyer straightened up and saw the rider appear. The man came to a halt and Fargo saw Barton Spender swing from the saddle and stride to the wagons.

"You idiot," he spat at Jack Breyer. "You had to pick that spot to do it? You wiped out five of the Davison's best side-wheelers and sank twenty other boats. Jesus, don't you have any damn sense?"

"I didn't think it would happen like that," Breyer said. "It wasn't my fault."

"What do you mean it wasn't your fault? You set the boiler to blow, goddammit," Spender threw back.

"Garret told me to do it the first chance I got. I asked him what if there were other boats around. He said to forget about the other boats and just get it done," Jack Breyer said.

Fargo saw Barton Spender's lips tighten. "Damn that kid. Isn't he ever gonna learn to think things through?" Spender asked, plainly upset. Fargo frowned as he turned Barton Spender's rhetorical question in his mind. The words shimmered inside him, digging at him, disturbing, unsettling. But he didn't know why and he frowned in thought as Judy's voice broke into his musings.

"They're just standing around. Why?" she asked.

"They're waiting for someone or something," Fargo said, scanning the men. Barton Spender walked to the canvas sacks, pulled the drawstring open on each and examined the contents, finally putting them all back in place. The sun passed the mid-afternoon mark and Judy leaned against Fargo as he stayed beside a tree, watching and waiting. Once again, he caught the sounds of hoofbeats before anyone else and pressed a hand on Judy's arm.

"Company," he breathed and she sat up at once. The riders appeared moments later, six men, one in a tailored riding jacket, a white shirt and a gray cravat, the others in range riding clothes. All carried guns, Fargo noted, the man in the riding jacket sporting a big Walch superimposed load Navy revolver with two hammers, two triggers and six chambers double-loaded for twelve shots. The newcomers reined to a halt and Barton Spender stepped forward to meet the man in the riding jacket and cravat.

"Mister Murphy," he said, a note of deference in his voice. The man swung from his horse and Fargo saw that on the cravat he wore a diamond stickpin. He had graying hair, a big head, a strong nose, and dark eyes that took in everything with one quick glance. "We're all ready, as usual," Spender said.

"And as I expected you'd be," the man said and stepped briskly to the wagons. He opened each sack, put a hand inside each and when he'd finished with the last his hand glistened with a yellow sheen. He motioned to one of the other men who dismounted, fished in a leather bag at the rump of his horse and came out with an assayer's scale which he carried to the wagons. Each canvas sack was weighed and the man called Murphy made notes on a scrap of paper. When the weighing was finished, Murphy took a piece of paper from inside his jacket, signed it and handed it to Barton Spender. Murphy and each of the five men with him took a sack back to their horses. "Done and finished for now," Murphy said to Barton Spender who nodded and watched as the man rode off with the others.

"Let's go," Spender said to Jack Breyer. "We'll leave the wagons in Memphis as usual and you men get your horses. I've seen a hell of a lot smoother trips." He climbed onto his horse and the others followed as he rode north.

Judy waited till they were out of sight before she spoke, her eyes peering south to where the six newcomers had ridden away. "Who were they? How do they fit in?" she asked.

"Damned if I know," Fargo muttered.

"It figures he'd sell the gold dust. I guess they were the buyers," Judy ventured.

"Legitimate gold buyers work out of an office, usually a bank. They don't meet in the middle of nowhere and bring their own scale. Something's wrong with all of it," Fargo said.

"How do you mean?"

"I'm not sure but I've a bad feeling," Fargo said and put his hands on her shoulders. "Look, I don't know what I'm going to do but I can't do anything while worrying about you. I want you to get out of here, go back and visit Sam Walker."

"I could help," she said.

"By being safe," he told her. "You've more than enough friends to get a ride back. Go and wait. I'll come get you." She tried to protest but his eyes stopped her and she kissed him beside her horse.

"Maybe we should just let it go, forget about it," she said. "I'm afraid for you."

"We can't. They won't let it go, not while you're still able to look for the truth," he said.

"You were right about Garret Davison being behind it," she said. "I guess I was wrong about Annabelle. You kept saying so."

"I did," Fargo said. "Now get out of here." He slapped the filly on the rump and sent her on her way, waited a few moments and climbed onto the Tobiano. He put the horse into a fast canter and followed the hoofprints of the six horsemen. But he felt the grimness wrapping itself around him as he rode, disturbing words coming back to him, certainties that were no longer certain.

7

The dusk had begun to turn to dark when he caught up to the six riders. He slowed, stayed back and saw them stop to bed down beside a forest of bur oak. Fargo noted that the boss man, Murphy, gave the orders. He had the six canvas sacks put together and chose one of the men to stand guard. "We'll change off every four hours," Fargo heard him say as one of the men sat down against a tree trunk with the sacks in front of him. The others took out blankets and lay down in a semicircle, Murphy going off by himself. The night set in and the men slept quickly, except for the one guarding the sacks.

Fargo stayed in a clump of trees as the moon climbed the velvet-blue sky. The plan took shape in his mind as he waited and he felt a grim smile edge his lips. It might not answer all the new questions that had come up but he wagered it would set the wheels in motion. And it had an edge of poetic justice to it. The idea grew more appealing as he half-dozed and let the hours go by. He snapped fully awake when one of the men took over guard duties for the other and Fargo let another hour go by before he rose and began to move through the trees. Making his way in the thickness of the bur oak, he circled the sleeping figures on steps careful and silent as those of a mountain lion.

Finally he was directly behind the man on guard in front of the six sacks. Edging forward, he drew the Colt from its holster, crept closer, the guard's thick neck only a foot away from him. The man never felt the revolver barrel smashing down onto his head. He toppled sideways as though he were a rag doll and Fargo caught him before he hit the ground, lowering him silently, almost gently. The blow had been hard enough to keep him unconscious until the dawn came, only an hour or so away. Fargo cast a glance at the others and made certain they all slept before he picked up the first of the sacks. He carried them, two at a time, into the forest where he had left the horse. When he had all six sacks together, he took a short-handled spade from his saddlebag, stepped behind one of the trees and began to dig alongside the trunk. When he had dug a large enough hole, he put the sacks inside it and covered the place with the earth, carefully putting back the grassy topsoil.

Taking the double-edged throwing knife from its calf holster, he marked the tree trunk, drawing a series of lines that would look like a cat or a bear had sharpened its class. He put the knife away as the first streaks of dawn touched the sky and returned deeper into the forest where he stretched out on his stomach and waited. It was a wait of only a half hour when the guard regained consciousness and slowly sat up. He felt the top of his head and let out an oath that combined pain and surprise. He pulled his hand down and looked at the blood on his fingertips, let out another loud oath and pushed himself to his feet. The others woke at once and Fargo watched Murphy sit up, jump to his feet and stride to the guard.

"The gold," he blurted out. "Where are the goddamn sacks?"

"Somebody hit me from behind," the man said, gingerly patting his head with a kerchief. "I didn't hear him, didn't see him."

"Goddammit," Murphy swore. "Son of a bitch."

"Who?" one of the others asked.

"Who the hell do you think?" Murphy said, spinning in a half-circle. "Who knew we had the gold? Who knew which way we were going?"

"Davison's people," one of the others said.

"That's right, the stinkin' bastards. Well, they're not getting away with it," Murphy said. "We're going to get the goddamn gold back. Get yourselves together. We'll pick up another few men on the way."

"We goin' to try and catch up to them?" someone asked.

"No, they've too much of a head start. We'll go right to the Davison place and get my goddamn gold back," Murphy said as he strode to his horse.

Fargo stayed prone, peering through the brush and trees but knew he was relatively safe. Murphy wasn't looking for anyone nearby. He was convinced the gold was on its way back to the Davisons and Fargo allowed a thin smile to cross his face. It had gone exactly as he expected it would. The wheels had been set in motion. Now he had to be certain to be on hand for the conclusion. He waited, unmoving, as Murphy and the others gathered themselves and rode away before he pushed to his feet and retrieved the Tobiano. He rode north, set a steady pace but didn't push the horse. Murphy and the others would stop to take on more men, and they'd have a night to sleep. Fargo estimated his pace, allowing for sleep himself, would bring him to the Davison Manor at least an hour before Murphy would arrive, and he spent a good part of his journey turning over how he'd fit himself into the explosion that was certain to take place.

Annabelle swam through his thoughts and it was with a grimness that he decided he'd see to her first. Garret and the others could fend for themselves, he grunted. Taking a path near the river, he passed Cairo and saw the waterfront still littered with the results of the carnage. He stayed within sight of the river as he rode and camped beneath a stand of honey locust when night came. In the saddle again with the dawn, he rode on, confident he was ahead of the others yet keeping an eye out nonetheless. The day had begun to move toward its end when he made a wide circle and passed through Benton's Landing before heading down to the Davison Manor. Fargo rode along the waterfront wharves, his eyes casually passing over the various figures waiting on the wharves, some to board, others collecting packages.

The frown dug into his brow as he saw one figure and he reined to a halt and dismounted. The figure waited beside a bollard, leaned on a single crutch and wore a wide swath of bandages wrapped around his upper torso. "Aren't you Annabelle Davison's exercise boy? Josh . . . ?" Fargo asked the youth.

"Yes, sir," the boy said, wincing as he tried to straighten up.

"What are you doing here? I thought you'd be laid up for at least a month," Fargo asked.

"Miss Annabelle fired me," the youth said.

"Fired you?" Fargo echoed in surprise.

"She said if I couldn't work the horses for her there was no reason to keep me on. She said she didn't pay people for doing nothing," the boy said. "She said when I was able to work again I could come back and apply for a job."

"That was big of her," Fargo said and the youth shrugged. "So where are you going now?"

"St. Louis. I've family there where I can rest up," Josh said.

"Good luck, son," Fargo said and returned to the Tobiano. When he rode on the sadness settled over him again and he felt almost sorry for everyone that touched on the Davisons. The daylight still held when he slowed as he reached the manor house, his eyes sweeping the property. Murphy and his men hadn't arrived. It was far too quiet for that and he rode to a halt at the big columns and dismounted. Annabelle stepped from the house, rushing toward him and took his hands in hers as she searched his face.

"My God, where have you been? You don't know how worried I've been about you," she said. "You heard about the disaster at Cairo, I take it." He nodded and she linked arms with him as she led him into the house. "We lost five of our finest vessels. I was afraid you might've been on one of them."

"I was there. I was lucky," Fargo said. He glanced across the room to see Garret Davison watch him enter, surprise and dismay in his eyes. Fargo smiled pleasantly at him and saw Garret's lower lips twitch. "Where's your boy?" Fargo asked.

"Barton?" Garret frowned.

"That's right."

"He's at the men's quarters," Garret said.

Fargo allowed a long, reluctant sigh. "I

shouldn't take sides," he said slowly. "But I'll make an exception. You're about to be attacked by your good friend Murphy and his friends." Fargo smiled again as he saw Garret Davison's jaw drop, alarm and surprise flooding his face.

"What are you talking about?" he asked, his lip quickly twitching.

"Attacked. You know about attacks. He's coming to kill you. You know about killing people," Fargo said.

Garret Davison swallowed hard as he leaped to his feet. "This some kind of bad joke?" he frowned.

"Not unless you get a laugh out of bullets," Fargo said.

"I've got to get Barton," Davison said and streaked for the door.

"Wait. What's all this about?" Annabelle cut in but her brother was already out the door and she turned to Fargo. "I'd like an explanation," she said.

"Later," he said. "You've a back room. Get in it and stay there." She hesitated, frowned at him. "Now, dammit," he said. "We'll do our talking after the shooting stops." The last words had just left his lips when the thunder of hooves resounded. Annabelle started to edge toward another room to the rear and Fargo turned away from her as he heard Garret Davison's voice, then Barton Spender and the running of footsteps. Both men burst into the house, Spender first and Fargo saw close to a dozen men following, each with a rifle or six-gun in hand.

"Pick a spot, behind the columns, at the corners of the house," Spender shouted. Fargo dropped to one knee as he drew the Colt. He could see through the open doorway to the dusk outside where Murphy and at least a dozen riders rode to a halt and spread out. Murphy dismounted and the other men did also, dropping low to the ground behind shrubbery and small trees that dotted the lawn.

"Where's the gold, you son of a bitch?" Murphy called out.

Fargo saw Garret Davison and Spender look at each other. "What the hell is he talking about?" Garret asked and Spender shrugged. Fargo moved to a window at the side of the house.

"Give it up or I'll kill every damn one of you," Murphy called.

"We don't have the damn gold," Spender called back.

"Fire!" Murphy's voice roared and a hail of shots erupted. Fargo ducked low as bullets slammed into the interior of the house, shattering windows and smashing lamps and vases. Spender's men began to return fire and Fargo saw Spender crouched behind one of the thick columns. He caught a glimpse of Jack Breyer at the right corner of the house. Garret Davison was still inside, firing quick bursts through a broken window. The dusk turned to dark and Spender's men were suddenly getting the best of the pitched battle. Four of Murphy's men lay dead on the lawn and the others were retreating to a line of hawthorn. Annabelle had followed his orders to stay in the rear of the house, he noted and another fast survey let him glimpse Barton Spender dart from the house, roll across the grass and come up firing. Fargo saw two of the attackers go down and Spender get up and weave his way across the lawn, letting the new darkness help cloak his way.

"No," Fargo bit out as Spender crashed through a hedge. Fargo ran to a side window, swung long legs over the sill and dropped to the ground. Wild gunfire still echoed from the front of the house as he raced to the hedge, hurled himself through it and glimpsed Barton Spender at the stable. Spender had no more idea than any of the others what had happened to suddenly blow things apart but he wasn't about to stay around to find out. He wasn't a man to stay aboard a sinking ship. Rat-like, he was racing to escape with his skin intact. As Spender disappeared into the stable, Fargo raced across the stretch of lawn.

Spender had been the one who'd plunged the knife into the government agent, Fargo was certain. Garret Davison hadn't the guts for it. He hadn't the guts for much of anything, Fargo had decided. Reaching the stable, Fargo burst through the ajar door and saw Spender beside one of the stalls. The man spun, six-gun in hand, and Fargo flung himself sideways in a twisting dive. Spender fired and as he hit the floor, Fargo heard the sound of a trigger hammer hitting an empty chamber. Fargo rolled, started to regain his feet as Spender hurled the gun at him with a curse of frustrated fury. Fargo ducked away from the hurtling weapon and saw Barton Spender run into one of the stalls behind him. Fargo fired two shots that sent splinters of wood from the stall door and heard his third shot fall on his own empty chamber.

He swore as he ran forward to the stall, had almost reached it when the door flew open and Barton Spender charged out carrying a three-pronged pitchfork. His face contorted in rage, he continued to charge forward, the pitchfork thrust out in front of him. Fargo tensed powerful calf muscles, forced himself to hold his ground as the three sharp prongs came at him. With the timing of a cougar, he waited another split second and then twisted and he flung himself sideways. He felt one prong of the pitchfork tear through the sleeve of his shirt as the weapon hurtled past him. Planting one foot solidly, he whirled and brought up a short right hook that landed hard at the bottom of Spender's ribcage. The man grunted and stumbled, and Fargo had the chance to bring around a powerful left thrown with all his strength behind it. The blow landed in the small of Spender's back and the man uttered a cry of pain as he fell forward almost into the stall.

Fargo followed as Spender fell to one knee but managed to still cling to the pitchfork. Turning, Spender swung the weapon in an upward arc and Fargo had to duck backwards. It was enough time for Spender to regain his feet and instantly wield the pitchfork in a downward arc, aiming the prongs at Fargo's legs. Fargo threw himself backwards, slammed into the side of the stall and half-jumped, half-fell out the door. He let himself fall forward, aware Spender was at his heels and as he dove he heard the pitchfork prongs hurl into the wood flooring of the stable. He pulled his legs forward, pushed to his feet to see Spender struggling to pull the three prongs out of the wood. It all took a matter of seconds but it was enough time for Fargo to step in with a roundhouse left. The blow smashed into Spender's jaw just as he pulled the prongs free and he staggered backwards, the weapon half-raised. Fargo's following blow, a right hook, landed on the point of Spender's jaw and the force of it sent him stumbling backwards again, this time half-turned around. Fargo's left followed instantly, a straight blow driven with all his strength behind it. Spender flew forward, smashed into the wall of the stall and Fargo heard a gargled cry come from the man.

He took another step forward, his arm pulled back to deliver another blow, when Barton Spender staggered back, turned and Fargo saw the three prongs embedded in the man's chest, two coming out of his armpits. He had impaled himself when he smashed into the wall and he took a step, his mouth hanging open but no sound coming from it. His eyes stared, pupils dilated and then he began to crumple, started to fall on his face but the pitchfork stopped his fall. He hung there, looking like some strange puppet whose strings had broken. He finally toppled sideways, as stiff as the pitchfork that fell with him.

"That was for Will Brantly," Fargo said and turned away, strode from the stable into the dark outside. The gunfire had stopped, the wild, pitched battle over. The lawn in front of the manor house was strewn with bodies, dimly lighted by the lamps from the house that had escaped being shattered. Fargo glanced at the still forms as he made his way past. He saw Murphy, the man on his back, arms outstretched and he walked on. As he neared the house he recognized some of Spender's men. It had gone as he thought it would and he felt no remorse, not for any one of them. They had pretty much wiped each other out and he was certain the world would suffer no great loss for it. But there were still questions hanging. He'd been all wrong about some of it, he knew that now. The final answers were still waiting and he uttered a soft curse as he entered the house.

Annabelle was there against the backdrop of bullet-marked walls in the living room. Her green eyes took on instant excitement when she saw him and she rushed to him at once. "You're alive, thank God," she murmured, her lips brushing his. "Garret was wounded. I had one of the men take him to the doctor."

"Spender's dead," Fargo said.

"So's most everyone else," Annabelle said. "Now, would you like to tell me what this was all about. You seem to be the only one that knows."

"That's true, at least this part of it," he said. "But I think you can tell me about the rest."

Annabelle frowned at him. "Whatever are you talking about?" she asked.

"The killings, the sinkings, your brother, Barton Spender, you, all of it," Fargo said.

"Why would I know about that?" Annabelle questioned.

"It was all going on around you," Fargo slid at her and she nodded.

"Yes, whatever it is you're talking about," she said.

Fargo's smile was patient. "That's what I told Judy Simmons. That's what I thought," he said. "But it turns out I was wrong."

Annabelle's eyes peered at him, earnest concern in their green depths. "How were you wrong?" she asked.

"I thought it was Garret and Barton Spender doing it all on their own. I thought they were hoodwinking you. I really did," Fargo said.

Annabelle's hand tightened on his arm. "And now you don't?" she said.

"Now I know better. You see, I was convinced Garret and Spender were into something. I didn't know what it was at first, but I was sure you weren't part of it. It took a while to put it all together and when I found out about Star Shipping and the stolen gold dust I still saw Garret and Spender being behind all of it."

"What made you change your mind?" she questioned.

"Little things. When I heard that Garret had told Jack Breyer to blow up Judy's boat in the middle of all the others." He paused and enjoyed Annabelle's frown. "Nobody that damn dumb could've put together all the rest of it. Never. That took somebody both smart and strong and he's neither. That left only you, honey."

Annabelle studied him thoughtfully. "You were my only mistake," she said.

"Me?" Fargo frowned.

"Yes. I thought I could control you. I thought I could turn you away from Judy Simmons's wild stories. I thought it was working," Annabelle said.

"It was for a while. You put on a damn good act in bed," he said.

"That was no act. I enjoyed every minute," she said.

"Good. Some part of all this was real," Fargo said.

She continued to study him, her lips pursing. "Little things. Garret's stupidity," she said.

"There was one thing more," Fargo said and she waited with amused patience. "I met the kid, your exercise boy. I knew you were a strange mixture, fire and ice, caring and callousness. Firing the kid showed that the ice really ruled. It was like the last brush stroke on a portrait."

"One you didn't care for," she smiled.

"Not much," he nodded. "But there are two things I haven't made fit. Why? Hell, you own a big riverboat line. You've got all kinds of money. Why steal gold dust from the government? Why risk everything you've got? I could see Garret trying to make a bundle for himself but not you."

"It didn't start with me. It was Garret and his gambling. He lost so much in New Orleans that I'd have had to sell every boat to pay for his losses. He didn't have the money to pay so they came looking to me. I'd heard about the government repository. It offered the best way to get money fast."

"You set up the whole scheme to pay off the gamblers with the gold," Fargo said.

"Murphy was the main one," she said.

"You killed people and sank their boats rather than pay with any of your own assets," Fargo said, scorn in his voice and she shrugged. "Why didn't you ship the barrels on your own boats? Why'd you go to all the trouble of using the small independents? What sense did that make?"

She offered a somewhat smug smile. "We knew that there was no way to stop some of the gold dust from leaking out with the borax powder. We also knew government agents would be coming around to check every cargo on every ship."

"So if they found any gold residue along with the borax powder it wouldn't be on your ships. They wouldn't suspect you of any involvement," Fargo finished.

"Exactly. They'd come down on the independents. They were shipping all the cargos for Star Shipping. We'd be outside suspicion," Annabelle said and Fargo felt a grudging admiration.

"Real clever," he said. "And you staged the fake accidents and sank the ships after a certain number of shipments just to play safe."

"That's right. We didn't want government agents finding anything, not even on the independents. It was added insurance, you might say," Annabelle said.

"But now it's over, Annabelle. You may have had Tim Olson in your pocket but there's a U.S. marshal in St. Louis. We'll be paying him a visit. Garret, too," Fargo said.

"I don't think so," Annabelle smiled.

"Me neither," Garret Davison's voice said and Fargo turned, his hand going toward his holster when he saw the big Winchester pointed at him. He let his hand slide down to his side as he swore silently.

"Garret wasn't wounded. I had him stay out of sight. I was certain you'd be back in one piece. I'd too much faith in you for anything less," Annabelle cut in.

"I'm touched," Fargo muttered.

"You see, when you barged in and said we were going to be attacked I was really taken by surprise," Annabelle said. "But when I heard Murphy demand the gold I knew what had happened. It fit in. I'd wondered where you'd disappeared to for the last few days. You said you were at the disaster at Cairo. You managed to follow the gold dust delivery and somehow you stole the gold from Murphy."

"Go to the head of the class," Fargo said.

"I really underestimated you, Fargo," Annabelle said.

"Except in bed," he said.

"Except in bed," she agreed. "Now you're going to tell us where you hid the gold."

"I can't remember," Fargo said.

"You'd better if you want to stay alive," she said, her voice turning into ice.

"Telling you won't keep me alive. We both know that," he said.

"I'll give you my word," she said. Fargo's chiding smile was his answer.

"Damn you," Annabelle hissed.

Fargo's thoughts raced. He'd already made it clear he'd no trust in her word. But she understood deviousness. She understood greed. The unprincipled are always quick to accept the lack of principles in others. It was part of their contempt for others. "That gold will bring a lot of money," he said. "I might be willing to split it."

Annabelle's eyes narrowed on him. "I could just kill you and forget about it," she said. "That might be smarter."

"It might also be dumber," Fargo said calmly. "Half a loaf's better than none. Your half could replace the five ships you lost at Cairo." Her green eyes stayed on him, thoughts turning behind them. "Why don't you ask Garret's advice?" he said blandly.

"Shut up," she snapped and he chuckled. She wrestled with her thoughts a few moments longer before answering. "All right, fifty-fifty," she bit out. "How do we do this?"

"I'll get it and bring you your half," he said.

"Don't be smart," Annabelle hissed.

He let his brows lift. "You can trust me a hell of a lot more than I can trust you," he said.

"Because you're a man of principle?" she tossed back and he nodded. She made a wry sound. "That's exactly why I can't trust you."

"For Christ's sakes, let me shoot him and the hell with the gold," Garret interrupted.

Annabelle's eyes didn't move from Fargo. "Shut up, Garret. This whole thing's your fault. I'm not coming out of it empty-handed," she said. Her eyes bored into Fargo, suddenly becoming a darker green as she made her decision. "Enough.

You'll give us the goddamn gold," she said. "*Garret!*"

Fargo cursed as his hand went to the holster. But the rifle crashed down onto the back of his head. He felt his legs turn to rubber as he went down and the world disappeared.

8

When his eyelids fluttered open he blinked, and took a moment to focus on the soft yellow glow of the lamp and the beams of the cabin ceiling. The soft, rolling motion was pleasant, soothing, and he felt like closing his eyes again and going to sleep. But he forced his eyelids to stay open, turned his head and felt the pain at once. He tried to move his legs to sit up and found he couldn't. Ignoring the pain in his head, he managed to pull himself up enough to look down his body. His legs were bound together at the ankles. He tried moving his arms and felt the ropes dig into his wrists.

"Shit," he swore and kicked the end of the bunk with both feet. The cabin door opened at once and a man's head came into sight.

"He's awake," the man called and another figure stepped halfway into the cabin and Fargo recognized Jack Breyer.

"Bad pennies keep turning up," Fargo said.

"Son of a bitch. You won't be makin' many more smart-ass cracks," Breyer said and withdrew as another figure entered and Fargo saw the long, auburn-tinted hair sway in the lamplight.

"This won't get you the gold," Fargo said.

"It's a start. Jack met with Murphy a day's ride

south of Memphis. That's where you saw him deliver the sacks to Murphy," Annabelle said. "By the time we get there you'll talk. One of Jack Breyer's talents is to get people to talk. He's very good at it. Pain does wonders to loosen people's tongues."

"You're putting a real strain on our romance, honey," Fargo said.

"We'll see how long you refuse to talk," she said. "Garret's at the wheel, Jack Breyer's tending to the boiler and we have three more men aboard. You're on one of our small work boats and we're running without lights. In the morning we'll put in at a small cove and go on come night."

"Being real careful, aren't you?" Fargo commented.

"You can never be too careful. You reminded me of that. Then after we have the gold we have to arrange an accident for you. No last minute sloppiness, no questions," she said.

"Wouldn't expect anything less of you, darling," he said. "I suppose you have my gun."

"In my bunk," she said. "Now you think about saving yourself a lot of pain and telling us where the gold is."

"I will. Promise," he said and she closed the door to the cabin as she left. He cursed softly and stretched out on the bunk. The double-edged throwing knife was in his calf holster and he drew his legs up, tried to bring his hands down to reach it but succeeded only in nearly falling off the bunk. He lay back, began to twist his wrists in an effort to slip out of the ropes. He stopped when he felt the blood on his wrists. They had knotted the ropes securely. He waited, gathered strength back and extended his legs across the top of the bunk and attempted to rub the ankle ropes loose. But the wooden top ledge of the bunk was too smooth and his ankles only slid from it. He waited again, decided he'd try to leave the bunk and he had just swung both bound legs over the side when the door opened. Annabelle stood there, a small, sinewy man beside her. She swept his figure as he sat perched on the edge of the bunk.

"I'll be dammed," she said. "You've been spending your time thinking about the wrong things. We can't have that." She motioned to the small man. "Tie him down," she said and the wiry figure hurried to the bunk with a length of lariat in hand. He pushed Fargo's legs back onto the bunk and proceeded to wrap the rope around his legs and waist, running it under the bunk until he had Fargo strapped and immobile. "Now you'll have nothing to think about except how much pain you'll be feeling if you don't tell us where the gold is," Annabelle said and left the little cabin with the man.

"You've a one-track mind, honey," Fargo called after her and cursed silently as the door closed. He lay back, all too aware there was nothing else he could do. But he made one decision. He wouldn't give her the pleasure of watching him be tortured. He'd buy a little more time and hope for a sudden chance. She'd have him killed once he told her where the gold was. But not immediately. She was too wily for that. Her devious mind would wonder if he'd play a final trump card and lie to her, letting death have the last laugh. She'd hold off killing him until she had the gold in hand. That was the time he'd buy. Not a hell of a purchase but then he didn't have much in the way of currency. His decision made, he let himself sleep.

The day woke him and he could see out a small, high window in the far wall. His restricted view let him see the heavy fronds of weeping willows that draped over at least part of the boat. They had pulled in where the thickly overhanging willows helped to hide the boat, not that it would be much noticed anyway. He lay still until the door of the cabin opened and Annabelle entered, Jack Breyer with her. "I hope you spent the night thinking," she said.

"I spent the night having to go," Fargo said.

Annabelle called out and the wiry-built man appeared. "Get Ruskin and take our friend to the bathroom. Keep his ankles tied," she said and stepped back as Fargo was unstrapped from the bunk and his wrists untied. The three men took him outside where they let him relieve himself over the side of the vessel. His eyes took in the boat, saw that it was a stern-wheeler and indeed small, a single iron chimney, the sides not more than six inches above the water. He also quickly noted that the boat was moored to a single low-hanging willow by one line. But the three men kept six-guns trained on him and when he finished, they bound his wrists again and escorted him, hobbling, back to the cabin.

They put him onto the bunk and again strapped him in, Annabelle looking on. "I suppose I should feel complimented," Fargo said. "You're taking no chances with me."

"Definitely not," she said.

"I'm going to make your life easy for you," Fargo said. "I'm not much for pain."

"I'm surprised. I saw you as the stalwart type who'd play the martyr," she said.

"Wrong again," Fargo said. "I'll tell you where the gold is but only when we get near to it and you untie me. I want a chance to run," he said.

"I untie you after I see the sacks," she said.

He shrugged. "You've all the cards," he said.

"You've another night of traveling before we get near the place. I'll take you to it when we get there."

She turned away and started from the cabin, the three men following her. "Keep the door closed. Look in on him every hour. If you have to take him up again make sure all three of you are there," she said and Fargo watched the cabin door close. He had bought another twenty-four hours. He could only hope to find a chance for freedom. He lay on the bunk and watched the weeping willow fronds hang straight in a windless day. They looked in on him every hour and one time Garret Davison appeared, his weak face gloating.

"You're lucky you're dealing with my sister. She's kinder than I am," he said.

"She's smarter than you are," Fargo tossed back and Garret Davison's face darkened at once.

"I'm looking forward to shooting you," Davison said.

"That makes us even," Fargo said and enjoyed Garret Davison's instant nervousness. Keeping Davison off balance could be valuable. People nervous and off balance made mistakes.

Garret licked his lips. "You won't be getting a chance to shoot me," he said.

"Don't be too sure," Fargo smiled and saw Garret Davison's face twitch.

"Bastard," Garret spit out as he almost rushed from the cabin. Fargo stretched and allowed himself a twinge of satisfaction. The day dragged on and Annabelle made another visit.

"I'm hungry," Fargo said.

"You can eat all you want after I have the gold," she said. "It'll be dark in an hour and we'll get under way again. You better deliver come morning."

"Count on it," he said and she speared him with a hard glance before she left. The dark settled down and Fargo felt the slow roll of the boat as it got under way, the sound of the paddle wheel a steady thump of wood against water. The moon rose, found its way through the small, high window into the cabin and he fought away a wave of despair. Time was on its way to running out. He'd only come up with one plan. They'd have to untie him for him to go to the gold. He'd insist on that and Annabelle would agree. She'd have six guns on him, including her own. The throwing knife was his one chance. He'd have to use it to get a gun in his hands. He closed his eyes and dozed and knew he was clinging to a thin thread of hope.

The moon rose higher, its pale rays filtering into the cabin and he'd just dozed off again when he snapped awake. The sound came to him, a faint click, the cabin door opening. He saw the dark shape move toward him and cursed his helplessness. A hand reached out, covered his mouth and he felt the softness of it. His brows lowered and he strained his eyes, saw the outline of soft brown hair cut short. "It's me," she said and drew her hand back.

"Judy," he gasped. "How in hell . . . ?"

"I told you I can feel when there's trouble. I proved that already. I'm proving it again," she said. "I felt it. I knew it, all the time after you left me."

"There's a knife on my right calf. Get it out and cut me loose while you talk," he said. Judy reached down, lifted his pant leg and drew the blade out and began to cut his ankle bonds. "I couldn't stop this feeling I had and I rode to the Davison place," she whispered. "But there was a terrible gunfight going on. I couldn't get close enough, then I saw you go into the house and then they carried you out." She cut through the ankle ropes and he swung from the bunk as she began to sever the wrist ropes. "I couldn't do anything but I watched and I followed, got myself a raft and poled my way after this work boat."

The wrist ropes parted and he hugged her to him. "Thank God for those visions of yours," he whispered. "But how'd you get into the cabin?"

"I swam on board and hid until the others were asleep. I got to the cabin and saw Jack Breyer on guard and knew you had to be inside. He left to get himself a drink of water and I sneaked in," Judy whispered. "I'm sure he's back outside again."

"Lay down on the bunk. I want him to see a body there," Fargo said and Judy swung onto the bunk and turned on her back. Fargo, the double-edged blade in hand, went to the side of the cabin beside the closed door. He thumped his foot on the floor and the door flew open at once. Jack Breyer burst in, six-gun in hand, his eyes focused on the form in the bunk. He stared, started closer when Fargo came up behind him and pressed the point of the blade against the back of his neck. "Drop the gun or this goes out the other side of your neck," he growled. Breyer stiffened, stayed in place and Fargo pressed harder. The man let the gun fall from his hand and Fargo's blow smashed into the back of his neck. It knocked him into the cabin wall. As Jack Breyer hit the side of the cabin, Fargo scooped the gun from the floor. He looked up to see the man drawing a second gun from inside his shirt. Fargo fired and Breyer's hand was still inside his shirt trying to draw the gun when he hit the floor.

The shot had split the silence of the night and Fargo cursed as he ran from the cabin. "Stay here or you'll catch a stray bullet," he yelled to Judy as she swung from the bunk. He ran from the cabin and heard the shouts and pounding footsteps. Garret was probably at the wheel and he'd stay there, at least for the moment, Fargo felt as he ran along the port deck. The small, wiry figure charged out of the center of the boat, fired and Fargo felt the shot graze his back. He threw himself forward, hit the deck and the man's next two shots were wild. Fargo came up against a water keg and fired while on one knee as the man ran toward the gunwale. He had almost reached it when the gun barked and he stiffened, staggered, fell forward and toppled over the low side of the boat. He hit the water with a loud splash as Fargo caught a glimpse of the figure coming toward him, crouched low along the boat's midsection. He waited, moved further behind the thick, round water keg, his eyes on the shadowy form. Suddenly the man erupted into action, racing toward the side of the ship, firing his gun as he ran, spewing a fusillade of shots.

Fargo stayed low as some of the shots thudded into the water keg and sent little fountains of water spouting into the air. But the man had reached the side of the ship with a last flurry of shots. He leaped in a dive as Fargo took aim, fired, and saw the figure jerk in midair before landing in the river. He waited, saw the man float facedown in the water before sinking from sight. Rising from his knee, Fargo swore as he heard the splash from the other side of the boat. The third hired gun had decided to escape with his life. He'd keep swimming, Fargo was certain and he moved toward the small pilot house. Garret and Annabelle were the only ones left and his eyes swept the boat as he moved forward. The pilot house was not raised as on the large riverboats but was on the deck level. Fargo saw Garret Davison still at the wheel but he held a revolver in one hand.

He half-crouched behind the spokes of the big wooden wheel and Fargo saw the fear in his face, his lips twitching as he peered forward. He'd heard the shots, of course, but he'd no way of knowing what they signified. Fargo crouched at the edge of the pilot house and let silence drape itself over the boat. He moved on cat's steps to the far side of the pilot house where he could also see down the deck. The seconds ticked off and Fargo knew they seemed like hours to Garret Davison, who was unable to sort out the explosion of gunfire and now the silence. But Fargo's eyes peered along the deck also. The silence held a question for him too. Annabelle had wrapped herself in silence. Only the thump of the paddle wheel broke the silence and Fargo's eyes were on Garret Davison as the man cracked.

"Annabelle, where are you, goddammit?" Garret screamed. "What the hell's happened?" Fargo stayed unmoving and there was no sound from Annabelle. Smart, Fargo grunted, the only smart one. She was using silence just as he was. But it was a standoff he couldn't let go on. Delay meant risks, the unexpected, a mistake, anything. Garret's voice cut into his thoughts again. "Annabelle? Answer me," the man called.

"Talk to him, Annabelle," Fargo said, lifting his voice. "I'm here by the pilot house. Join me." Again, there was only silence. "I've got Garret in my sights. I'm deciding whether I'll shoot him through the second and third spokes of the wheel or the first and second," Fargo said in a conversational tone. "Got any preferences?"

"Oh, Jesus," Garret's voice cut in, a hoarse cry.

"Stay at the wheel, Garret," Annabelle's voice said. "I'm here in the stern, by the paddle wheel, Fargo. I've got your little friend Judy." Fargo heard his own gasped curse as he straightened up. "You shoot Garret and she goes into the paddle wheel."

"Back off," Fargo said and strode along the narrow side of the vessel to the stern. He stopped at the corner of the rear housing and felt the warmth of the boiler fire. He saw Annabelle, one arm around Judy's neck, the other holding a gun pointed at her cheekbone.

"I stayed in the cabin, Fargo," Judy called. "I did what you told me."

"Yes, she did, good little thing that she is," Annabelle said. "When I heard the first shot I knew two things. You'd gotten free and you couldn't have done it alone. So while the others were running around to get you I went to the cabin and there she was."

Fargo's eyes went to the paddle wheel as it churned the water only inches behind Judy. "What's your deal?" he said.

"I still want the gold. Tell me where it is or she goes into the paddle wheel," Annabelle said, her voice ice. "You ever see anybody fall into a paddle wheel? They don't die right away. They get knocked around, tossed up and hit and carried along and hit again. Their bones break first, legs, arms, chest. Sometimes their heads go off."

"Sounds like you've watched often," Fargo said as his thoughts raced desperately. It'd only take one shove to push Judy over the low rail and into the paddle wheel. His eyes were narrowed as he stared at the two figures. Annabelle was a head taller than Judy and she was standing very still. A single shot could do it, he murmured inwardly. But it would have to be absolutely dead on target.

The slightest thing to cause him to miss would end Judy's life and he grimaced as he thought about using a stranger's gun when he needed the absolute accuracy of his Colt. But he had little choice, he realized. He started to bring the gun up when the boat shuddered as it slid over a sandbar and he had to sway to keep his balance. He cursed as he lowered the gun, the decision made for him.

He straightened and stepped out onto the rear deck and walked toward Annabelle. "That's close enough," she said, keeping her gun against Judy's cheek. Fargo took another two steps closer. "Don't play with me," Fargo," she said and pulled the hammer back on the revolver.

"Wouldn't think of it," Fargo said.

"Put the gun down and slide it over here," Annabelle ordered. He obeyed, sending the gun slithering toward her with a push of his foot. This was the last chance, the split second he'd have to take. Annabelle bent down to pick up the gun. For a brief, fleeting instant her gun was away from Judy's cheek. Fargo dived forward as Annabelle picked the gun up from the deck. "Goddamn," he heard her hiss as she swung her own gun around and he felt the heat of the flash against his cheek as he dived into her. He went in low, slammed into her at just below the knees and she went down backwards. His chopping blow to her wrist sent her gun flying from her hand and he felt a sharp pain in his groin as she kicked out. He fell to one side, seeing her scramble to regain her feet. She was almost upright when she slipped, her left foot going out from under her.

She tried to regain her balance but she went over sideways, her ankles crashing into the low rail. Fargo dived for her as she went over the rail, his hand catching a piece of her blouse. It tore and his lips drew back as she went headfirst into the paddle wheel. She screamed, a terrible wail, and he looked away. "Oh, God," he heard Judy gasp. Annabelle's scream trailed off into a quick succession of gargling sounds and ended abruptly as the churning sound of the paddle wheel took on an added thud. Fargo heard the pounding of footsteps and scooped the gun from the deck as Garret Davison came charging down the port deck. Gun in hand, Garret Davison fired wild shots from in front of his handsome, weak face now contorted into a screaming mask.

Fargo fired two shots and Garret Davison clutched at his chest as he stumbled forward, his momentum carrying him past Fargo's crouched figure. He fell sprawling on the deck at the edge of the paddle wheel, one hand outstretched as though he were trying to reach the churning paddles. He twitched and lay still, fingers curled around the low rail. Fargo rose and then Judy was in his arms, clinging fiercely to him. He walked to the pilot house holding his arm around her waist until she stopped trembling. "What now?" she asked.

"Unfinished business," he said. "You want to pilot this thing to where I hid the gold?"

"No," Judy said firmly. "I want off this boat, as fast as I can. My raft's back a few miles. We can get it." He nodded and understood and Judy took the wheel as he went to retrieve his Colt. She steered the boat onto a flat expanse of shore and shut down the engine. Fargo swung from the craft with her into the shallow water and she held his hand all the way back on the long walk. He held her again when they reached the raft.

"Thanks for coming for me. Thanks for those visions of yours," he told her.

"Thanks for believing in me from the beginning," she said and he poled the raft into midriver and they sailed down the Mississippi under the moon that had reached the end of the sky. It was morning and bright sunlight when he dug up the ground where he'd hidden the sacks and she helped load them onto the raft.

"There's got to be a federal marshal in St. Louis," he said.

"There is," she replied and they rafted their way back. In Memphis, Judy found an old friend who gave them a ride to St. Louis. She waited on the boat while he went to see the marshal, who turned out to be a big, gruff man who knew Tim Olson. He listened to Fargo's tale of murder, greed, and duplicity and his face was grave when Fargo ended his story.

"Sorry about Tim," the marshal said. "But he's not the first lawman to go bad and he won't be the last. I did get a visit some weeks back from another government agent. He told me about the gold dust they were trying to find. He'll be mighty happy when I bring him these sacks."

"It's all in your hands now, Marshal," Fargo said.

The man fastened him with an appraising stare. "You wouldn't like to work for me, would you, Fargo?" he asked. "I could use someone like you."

"Thanks but maybe some other time. I've got trails to break," Fargo said and left after a handshake. When he reached the boat where Judy waited he saw her frown at the sack in his arms. "I held this one out," he said. "The government got most of their gold dust back, more than they thought they'd recover. You could say it's a kind of reward for getting their gold back to them. There's enough here for Captain Sam to replace the *Molly*

M. and for you to get a new boat, if you've a mind."

"I've a mind. The river's always been my life. It's all I know," she said and her lips pressed his. "For everything," she murmured. He went to the bank in Benton's Landing with her where she deposited the sack and she followed him to Doc Sawyer, where the Ovaro greeted him with a rush of excitement.

"He's fit as ever," the veterinarian said as Fargo returned the Tobiano and swung onto his horse and knew the reunion of old friends. Judy rode with him as they left and Fargo saw her look back to where the Mississippi curved its way in the distance.

"What are you thinking?" he asked.

"The river," she murmured. "It goes on, unaffected, timeless, above and beyond anything men and women can do. It goes on and lets us know how insignificant we are."

"There's a lesson there someplace," Fargo said and Judy brought her filly against the Ovaro, her eyes twinkling.

"I've another vision," she said. "Usually they concern trouble but not always."

"What's this one telling you?" he asked.

"It's telling me we're going to get away and make love until we're too exhausted to stand up," Judy said.

"Hell, that doesn't take a vision. I've been figuring exactly the same thing," Fargo said. She leaned over, kissed him and he led the way into the rich, green hills for another kind of reward.

LOOKING FORWARD!
The following is the opening
section from the next novel in the exciting
Trailsman series from Signet:

**THE TRAILSMAN #172
SUTTER'S SECRET**

---

*Hell's Picket, Wyoming, in 1860—
a two-bit town where frontier justice was swift
and the noose was always ready to swing a man . . .
even the wrong one.*

He'd seen worse.

The tall man reined in the black and white pinto at the top of a red bluff and sat looking down on the settlement. A couple dozen shacks and false-fronted lumber buildings stood below in the middle of the dry sage plain. The afternoon sun gilded the tin roofs and they glistened like gold. Even from this distance, he could see tiny figures, wagons, and horses raising small plumes of dust in the streets of the town. The winding red trail led into town and out again, away into the distance.

So this was Hell's Picket. In all his years riding the west, he'd seen a lot of shabby towns thrown up in the middle of nowhere. And he'd seen worse. His lake-blue eyes swept the horizon, taking in the rosy bluffs and distant peaks. Far above in the crystal sky, a silent eagle floated. He felt the tug of the open trail, the empty wild land that lay all around. As if reading his thoughts, the Ovaro shifted beneath him and stamped a hoof impatiently.

Fargo stroked the Ovaro's strong neck. We have a job to do, he told the animal silently. He pulled out a scrap of paper from his jacket pocket and reread the message that had somehow managed to reach him when he had been passing through Kansas City.

Mr. Fargo, it read. *I heard about you from Major Jack Lewis. He said you were the one if I ever needed help. I need it now. This thing's gotten too big for me and my boys to handle. If you can come, I'll meet you in Hell's Picket in Wyoming Territory on the first of July. Ask for Mack in the main hotel at sundown. I'll be able to pay you well.*

What the hell was it all about, Fargo had wondered. Who was this Mack character? And what was this about "my boys?" It sounded like a gang or a posse. His suspicions aroused, Fargo had sent off a telegram to his old friend Jack Lewis at Fort Reliance. But word came back that the Major had got himself killed in Indian action the week before. And with Major Lewis dead, there was no way to find out anything about this mysterious message. Now there was only one thing to do. He had to go see for himself.

The pinto started forward on the trail heading into town. Beside the trail, Fargo read the battered sign: WELCOME TO HELL'S PICKET, POPULATION 134 LAW-ABIDING CITIZENS. Fargo slowed the pinto to a canter and then a walk as they reached the first buildings. Lining the dusty streets were the usual collection of storefronts—an emporium with trail supplies and groceries, livery stables, sheriff's office, and courthouse, even a store that promised "Tables, Chairs, Beds, and Coffins—Made to Order."

Mountain wagons rumbled by, loaded with kegs, boxes of supplies, piles of sheep skins, and buffalo pelts. The drivers in their dusty clothes glanced at him with hard, wary eyes, their faces deeply lined by sun and weather. There were few women around and those he saw were dressed in homespun handmade bonnets to keep off the harsh sun. Ranching life was hard hereabouts. A family could scrape a living out of the cruel land, Fargo knew, but the reward for their hard work could rarely be counted in greenbacks.

A pudgy red-faced man was passing out handbills to passersby. He ran puffing up to Fargo and reached up, offering him one.

"We got a shootin' show in the main square this afternoon!" the man said. "A world famous shooter—"

Fargo shook his head and refused the handbill, riding on. He'd seen enough real shooting for a lifetime. And most professional shooters were nothing more than circus performers, magicians, and charlatans, their shooting tricks depending more on props and tricks than real shooting skill. There were very few exceptions.

He reached the center of town to find an open square fronted by the large ramshackle two-story Hell's Picket Hotel and Saloon. In the middle of the dusty square, Fargo noticed an elaborate platform, elevated ten feet above the ground with a wooden stair ascending. He could see the outlines of trapdoors in the platform. Above was the thick beam arm of the gallows and a couple of empty nooses swung in the breeze. He calculated there was room enough to hang half a dozen men at a time. With that hanging stage looking at you every day, a man would sure stay law-abiding, he thought.

He dismounted and tethered his pinto in front of the hotel. He turned about and spotted a building on the other side of the square. It was all gingerbread gables and filigreed shutters, garishly painted in bright pink and yellow. For a moment, Fargo smiled to himself, thinking it must be a fancy bordello, but then he saw the windows were boarded over and the front door closed. The huge sign, SAM BLADE'S CASINO swung by one nail. Businesses came and went on the frontier. Fargo idly wondered what had happened to that one.

" 'Scuse me, stranger," a deep voice said. Fargo turned to find himself face to face with a lanky fellow. His face was long and serious, and the skin hung in loose folds from his narrow face like an old dog's. A silver star was pinned to his leather vest.

"You must be sheriff of Hell's Picket," Fargo said, touching the brim of his hat.

"I am," the man said, not unfriendly but without a smile. "And who might you be?"

"Name's Skye Fargo."

The sheriff looked him over twice.

"I've heard of you," he said. Still no smile. "What brings you to town?"

Even though he had nothing to hide, Fargo didn't like questions. There was no telling who this Mack character he was supposed to meet was and what he was getting himself into. Instinct told him to say as little as possible before he found out the whole story.

"Just passing through," Fargo answered lightly, without hesitation.

"Hm," the sheriff nodded, his eyes still on Fargo.

"Why all the questions?" Fargo asked. "You expecting some trouble around here?"

"Nope," the sheriff said. "I just like to keep my eye on any strangers coming through. We're a law-abiding town. Like to keep it that way."

"Sounds good to me," Fargo said agreeably.

The sheriff seemed to relax at this and offered his hand.

"The name's Harry Sikes," he said. They shook.

"Nice place," Fargo said, glancing around the square. "What happened to your casino over there?" He pointed across the way to the gaudy pink and yellow building.

"Oh, a fellow named Sam Blade came into town and opened up that big place," Sheriff Sikes explained. "Did right well for a spell. Got a lot of gambling men coming through, some new fancy girls, that kind of a thing. No trouble though. Well-run place. Then the rumor went around that the tables were fixed and the game was crooked. Well, I say a man's not guilty till you prove it. And nobody ever rightly caught Sam Blade cheating anybody. But I guess those gamblers felt like they were losing too often and the gaming just dried up and went out of town again. Sam Blade went belly-up and left six months ago. We ain't seen him since."

There was a sudden commotion at the other end of the street and Fargo turned to see a figure riding hell-bent on a glistening palomino, both hands in the air, pistols blazing. The sheriff jumped and started to draw his gun.

"Oh hell, it's that shooting show," he said. He hurried away to the other side of the square. Fargo watched as the rider galloped expertly with blurring speed around the common, firing into the sky and shrieking like the very Devil, as the citizens of Hell's Picket came running toward the square shouting with excitement. Fargo grinned as he recognized Deadeye Dena. Hell, she was getting old but still up to her old tricks.

Suddenly, the whole town seemed to take on the atmosphere of a carnival as the crowd gathered and the palomino raced around and around. Deadeye Dena whooped again and stood on the saddle of her horse, holding the reins in one hand and firing into the air with the other. Then she reined in next to the gallows platform and a cloud of dust swirled around her. When it cleared, she was standing up on the platform and Fargo got a good look at her.

It had been a few years since he'd run into Deadeye Dena, the "Fastest Lady Shootist in the West." She hadn't changed a bit. Under her battered black hat, her sunburned, wrinkled face was as tough as old leather. Two silver braids hung down her back and traces of her Shoshoni heritage showed in her strong jaw and her black eyes. She was wearing a buckskin fringed dress on her wiry figure and silver-chased rattlesnake skin boots. Around her hips hung half a dozen holster belts with pistols of all kinds and two bullet-filled bandoliers crossed her chest.

Dena gave a bloodcurdling war whoop and doffed her black hat, tossing it in the air. She spun all the way around while she drew two long-barreled vaquero pistols and plugged the hat a dozen times. It fluttered to the ground, cut neatly in two pieces while the crowd cheered.

"Betcha can't do that with a nickel!" a tall man in the crowd shouted to her. "Everybody knows girls can't shoot."

"Got a nickel?" she said, her hand on one hip. "For every nickel I plug, you owe me one. For every nickel I miss, I give you two! And if you want to hop up here, I'll give you five nickels for every one you hit."

"Sold!" he said. The crowd laughed, eager to see the contest. The tall man climbed up the stairs and stood on the high gallows platform. He towered over the small figure of Deadeye Dena and she smiled up at him with all the sweetness of a rattler about to strike.

Fargo stood at the back of the crowd and watched as the tall man tossed nickels high in the air and Dena plugged them, one by one without fail. At first the man laughed as he handed over a nickel for every one she hit, but then his face became serious.

"It ain't so hard," he said, pulling out his gun.

"Toss a few for me and I'll show you how it's done."

Dena bent down and took a handful of nickels from her pile. She made sure he was ready, then tossed the first. It flew upward, high in the afternoon sky, glinting in the light. The tall man pulled the trigger and the coin fell to earth. The crowd made a circle around it.

"Ain't hit it," somebody said, tossing the coin back to Dena.

"Want to try again?" she asked. He tried three more times with no better luck. He was sweating. Then he threw nickels into the air for her again, and as the pile of nickels at her feet grew and he ran out of coins, the pile turned into greenbacks and he grew restless. He shook his head as if giving up. The crowd egged him on.

"Come on, Marvin!" one of the men shouted. "Her luck's gotta turn soon!" But Fargo knew it was more than luck. It was skill. Deadeye Dena had spent her lifetime looking down the barrel of a gun or a pistol and she could outshoot almost anybody in the West. Finally, the tall rancher had had enough.

"I quit!" he yelled, stomping off to the laughter of the crowd. "Must be some kind of a trick!"

Dena laughed too as she watched him go. Then she pulled a small hand mirror from her pocket. She turned her back to the retreating man and looked over her shoulder at his reflection in the mirror. Slowly, she raised her pistol and laid the barrel on her shoulder. A murmur went up from the crowd and a few men muttered as the women gasped.

"Don't," somebody said softly. The sheriff, standing to one side, started forward as if to stop her.

Dena pulled the trigger. Across the square, the tall man's hat flew off his head. He gave a yell and started to run, then turned back in a fury when he heard the crowd's laughter. He picked up his hat, beat the dust out of it and disappeared around a corner.

"Anybody else care to try?" Deadeye Dena said. There was a silence in the crowd. Nobody wanted to take her on. Dena glance at the pile of money at her feet and Fargo read her thoughts in her face. That was all the money she'd make on this show. The crowd started to drift away as Dena bent down to gather up the bills and coins.

"Sure, I'll take you on," Fargo said.

Dena glanced up at the sound of his voice and her face broke out in a big smile.

"Why, bless my bullets!" she said. "If it isn't Mr. Skye Fargo!" At the sound of his name, many in the crowd turned back to look at him curiously, muttering among themselves. His name and reputation had spread throughout the West. "What brings you to Hell's Picket?"

"Just looking for something to shoot at!" Fargo said with a big smile on his face as he climbed the stairs to the platform. "You care to take me on?" The crowd applauded.

"I'll play you plugged pennies for gold eagles," Fargo offered. Dena whistled.

"Gold eagles? You devil," she said. "You're on."

"I'm bettin' on Fargo!" a man in the crowd called out.

"Not me," another said. "I'm putting my money on the lady."

"Winner keeps ten percent," Fargo said.

"That's fair." It was the pudgy man Fargo had seen earlier handing out the flyers. "I'll keep track of the money. Give me your bets, men."

In a moment, there were two huge piles of greenbacks and gold eagles on the gallows platform. Fargo eyed them. Ten percent of the winnings would be a nice haul for one afternoon. For either one of them. Dena caught his glance and flashed him a grin.

"You ain't got a chance," she said in a tough voice, for the crowd's benefit. She tossed a penny high in the air and Fargo slipped the Colt from his holster, brought the barrel up fast and fired. The penny bounced in the sky and the audience whistled and cheered—the ones with money on Fargo, anyway.

Again and again, Dena and Fargo took turns tossing pennies and firing. Again and again, the coins fell to earth as mangled bits of metal. They shot right-handed, left-handed, standing on one foot, looking in a mirror, lying on their backs, every which way. Ten minutes became half an hour, then an hour. When the crowd ran out of pennies, somebody was sent over to the saloon to change a few greenbacks. It was clear the match was going to be a draw or it would go on all night. The crowd started to lose interest. One man stepped forward and demanded his bet back. Then another decided he'd had enough too. Fargo realized every time a man took his bet back, the game got less interesting to the ones left in it. Eventually, they would all take their money back. Something had to be done.

Dena threw a penny high in the air and Fargo took aim, then at the last second, he shifted the barrel and fired. The penny fell straight to earth.

"Goddamn it" Fargo swore in the heavy, startled silence. "Goddamn. I can't believe I missed."

Deadeye Dena flashed him an exasperated look as if to say, I saw you miss that shot on purpose. They shook hands.

The crowd went wild, at least the ones who had won their bets. They pressed forward as the pudgy man counted out ten percent of the winnings and handed them to Dena. Fargo and Dena pushed their way out of the crowd and wandered over to where her palomino was waiting.

"That wasn't fair and square and you know it," Dena said once they were out of earshot of anybody. She jingled her pockets, heavy with the loot. "You want half?"

"Hell no," Fargo said. "You keep it. Losing was better than letting all that money get up and walk away again. Why don't you join me for some dinner?"

"Haven't you got an offer from somebody your own age?" she teased him. "Nothing I like better than dining with the dashing Skye Fargo," she added. "But damn it, I promised I'd do a gig down in Cheyenne tomorrow morning. It's a big show and there's a promoter from back east going to be there. Might be a big break." She stamped her foot in exasperation. "I'd rather have a jaw wag with you and hear all your tales. But I'm running behind and I've got to ride all night to get there."

"Invitation's always open," Fargo said, disappointed. Too bad. It was never dull when Deadeye Dena was around. She mounted her palomino. She was one hard-driving woman, tough as pemmican but bighearted. He watched as she rode off and disappeared. The sun was lowering in the west and it was just before sundown. He wondered if Mack was watching inside the hotel.

The dilapidated lobby was furnished with shabby horsehair couches and two dead palms planted in spittoons. Behind the reception desk sat a bespectacled young clerk, his pale blond hair center-parted and slicked down. He was reading a newspaper.

"I'm looking for somebody named Mack," Fargo said.

The clerk continued reading and Fargo repeated the request a little louder. There was no response. Was the clerk deaf? Fargo reached across the counter and tapped the man on the shoulder. He nearly jumped out of his skin, and the newspaper flew everywhere.

"What do you want?" the clerk asked nervously as he gathered up the pages. Fargo repeated himself. The clerk adjusted his glasses and sat down again.

"Never heard of anybody named Mack," he said shortly. He buried his nose in the newsprint again. Fargo reached across the counter and grabbed the hotel registry. The clerk lowered his paper.

"Hey! Hey! You can't do that!"

"Just looking," Fargo said calmly, his eyes scanning the ink signatures of the hotel guests. Nope. No one with a name even close to Mack. Fargo handed the book back to the clerk, who snatched it away and returned to reading his paper.

Maybe if he sat and waited for a while, Fargo thought. Mack was sure to turn up. It was just on sunset. He settled down on one of the horsehair couches, which prickled him. He shifted around and decided he'd sat on rocks that were a whole lot softer. Why the hell did anybody make couches so damned uncomfortable? He slouched and pulled his hat brim down over his eyes. He could doze and still keep an eye out from time to time on whoever came through the lobby. The grandfather clock ticked. Nine o'clock came and went and the lobby was still deserted. Hell's Picket was a helluva quiet town.

At half past nine, Fargo heard horses pull up outside. He rose and pushed back his hat expectantly. There were several voices. Two men were arguing but he couldn't make out the words. The door swung open and in came a beefy black-haired man in fancy duds, his jinglebobs clattering on the floor. God, how he hated jinglebobs, Fargo thought to himself. The noisy oversized spurs made the sound of an approaching idiot. The big man wore a hat with a silver band and his broad shoulders and muscular arms strained against the dark fabric of his jacket.

Could this be Mack? Fargo didn't like the looks of him. He started to move forward, then hesitated as a couple entered. The young man, in rancher's clothes, was gaunt and angry-looking. Under his red hair his pale face was flushed with fury and he darted furious looks at the big fellow. On his arm was a young woman. Fargo's eyes ran appreciatively over her willowy form, the curves of her narrow waist and rounded hips poured into a yellow gingham dress. Her full breasts swelled over the top of the low cut bodice and her curling strawberry hair fell over her shoulders to her waist. With one hand, she clutched at the young man's arm, while the other nervously twisted a handkerchief. Her eyes were glued on the floor.

The big man banged on the counter to get the clerk's attention.

"Yes sir!" the clerk jumped up. "Oh, it's you, sir."

Obviously, the clerk knew the big guy. So he couldn't be Mack.

"Got my room?" the big man growled. "There's three of us."

"Certainly, sir. Room Three." The clerk handed him the key.

"Get my horses over to the livery," the big man said. He jerked his head toward the staircase and the young man and woman started up the steps. The big man followed, then noticed Fargo for the first time. He stopped and turned, staring him down. Behind him, the young woman raised her eyes and Fargo saw them for the first time. They were sad, suffering, and surrounded by dark circles. What the hell was wrong with her, he wondered. Maybe she was ill or in mourning for somebody. She noticed his gaze and she returned it, a flicker of interest passed and then she looked down again and leaned against the young man who held her arm.

"What're you looking at?" the big man growled. Fargo shrugged. No use starting trouble over nothing. "Who the hell is *he*?" the big guy shot at the hotel clerk. The clerk adjusted his spectacles and sniffed.

"Just some troublemaker passing through town," the clerk said.

The big guy turned away and continued up the stairs. The clerk left the lobby to take care of the horses. Fargo glanced at the clock. It was quarter to ten. Whoever Mack was, he hadn't shown. Fargo paced the empty lobby a few times, then decided to stable his horse for the night and take a room in the hotel. Even though he preferred sleeping out in the open, a long hot bath and a feather bed would be a welcome change. And if Mack did show up the next morning, he'd be right here. Fargo left the hotel, unhitched his pinto and took it down to the livery stable for the night where he found the hotel clerk. They walked back to the hotel together and the clerk checked him into a room.

"Room Two," the clerk said, pushing the registry book across the counter. "Sign right here." Fargo scribbled his name and read the name of the big man who had signed in just before him.

"Sam Blade," Fargo read aloud. "Is that the same Sam Blade who ran that casino across the way? The one that went out of business because rumor got around the games were fixed?"

"That's Mr. Blade" the clerk said stiffly.

"Who's the girl? And the other guy?" Fargo asked. The clerk's eyes widened with suspicion.

"None of my business," he said stiffly, picking up his newspaper.

"Yeah," said Fargo. He hoisted his saddlebag and ascended the stairs.

The room was comfortable enough, with a big brass bed that was plump and inviting. In the morning, Fargo decided, he'd call for a hot bath and have a big breakfast while he waited for Mack to materialize. He poured some water into the bowl on the washstand and was dashing the trail dust when he heard voices through the thin wall. A woman's voice, then a man's. Two men.

Normally, he didn't like messing in other people's business, but there was something in the tone that captured his attention. The woman's voice was plaintive, begging. She was in some kind of trouble. Fargo straightened up and pressed his ear to the wall. The words were muffled but he could make them out.

"Please, please don't, Mr. Blade," she sobbed.

It was Sam Blade and the woman and the young man he'd seen down in the lobby.

"He'll do as I say and shut up!" Blade's deep voice responded. "I've had about as much of his talk. Just remember what's going to happen if you don't cooperate."

There was the sound of a crash and a thud against the wall. The young woman screamed and a shot rang out, then another.

Fargo leapt to the door and ran into the corridor. He tried the knob of Room Three but it was locked. Inside he could hear the woman sobbing. He gave the oak door a swift kick, but it held. Fargo drew his Colt and fired at the lock twice. The metal shattered and he kicked again. The door flew open.

Fargo held his smoking Colt before him. Sam Blade stood, pistol in hand, looking down. At his feet lay the young man, shot in the head and chest, a pool of blood already spreading across the floor. Kneeling on the carpet beside the dead youth was the woman in yellow. She turned her grief-ridden face to him, then got to her feet and flung herself at him. Fargo caught her with one hand as she collapsed against him. He circled her waist with one arm. She was breathing fast, like a scared bird.

"Drop the gun," Fargo said to Blade.

Sam Blade glanced up and seemed to notice him for the first time. He shook his head as if to clear it, then slowly glanced at Fargo's Colt. For a long minute he stared at the gun, then he smiled. It was an ugly smile.

Behind him, Fargo could hear the pounding of feet on the stairs and voices calling out. Somebody came to the open doorway and gasped. It was the clerk, who took one look at the dead man on the floor and retreated.

"Murder! Murder!" the clerk shouted as he ran back down the stairs.

"I said drop it," Fargo repeated. "I'm not asking again."

Sam Blade shifted the barrel of his gun and aimed it at the woman in Fargo's arm. His black eyes glittered, never leaving Fargo's.

"Shoot me and my last act's going to be to pull this trigger. The bullet will rip right through that pretty flesh."

He was one cool customer, Fargo thought. Most men would have panicked, but Sam Blade knew just what card to play next. Fargo thought fast. If he pushed her off to the right and dove in the opposite direction, Sam might shoot and miss. Or he might not miss. If he fired at Sam's gun, he might throw off the shot. But maybe not. If he pushed her behind him, he could take the bullet himself. Fargo had just decided to do that, when he heard the approach of heavy footsteps.

Sheriff Sikes appeared in the door. The bespectacled clerk peered around the corner behind him.

"What the hell?" Sikes exclaimed, spotting the dead man. "Sam Blade! What's going on here?"

"Unhand the girl," Sam Blade growled, motioning with his pistol toward Fargo. She was trembling in his arm.

"The hell I will!" Fargo said. "Drop *your* gun!" In the doorway, Sheriff Sikes drew his pistol.

"Both of you drop 'em right now!" he barked. Sam Blade gave a smirk and threw his pistol onto the floor. Fargo followed suit. The woman sagged against him and Fargo steered her toward a chair. She sat, then buried her face in her hands. "Now, what's going on here?" the sheriff asked. "Blade, what are you doing back in town?"

"Just came in tonight to do some business," Blade said. "I went downstairs to fetch some . . . more water and I heard some shots. I came running back to find this . . . this bandit murdered Scotty MacKenzie!"

Sheriff Sikes glanced at Fargo and shifted the barrel of his pistol to cover him.

"That's not what happened," Fargo said.

"Step away from the girl," Sikes warned.

"Sure," Fargo said, moving away. "But that's not what happened. I was next door in my room when I heard them in here arguing. Next thing, I heard two shots and I came to find out what happened. The door was locked, so I shot the lock. Sam Blade's the one who killed him. Ask her," Fargo finished, gesturing toward the woman in yellow. "She was a witness."

"Well?" Sikes asked her. "What do you say, miss? What's your name?"

The young woman looked up, her tear-streaked face twisted with pain.

"Julie," she said softly. "Julie MacKenzie."

She glanced at the dead man on the floor, then at Fargo. She opened her mouth to speak. Sam Blade cleared his throat loudly. Julie looked at Blade for a long moment, turned bright red and looked down at the floor.

"He did it," Julie said quietly. "He killed my brother."

"Who did it?" the sheriff asked, his voice short. "Sam Blade?" She shook her head no, her face hidden by her hair. "Then this other fellow, Skye Fargo? He did it?" There was a long pause and she nodded yes, but would not look up.

"She's lying," Fargo said. "I don't know why, but she's covering up for Sam Blade." Blade's black eyes were hard as steel.

"That's your story," Sheriff Sikes put in. "This your gun?" He picked up Fargo's Colt and sniffed it. He opened the chamber and looked inside. "Two bullets missing." Sikes walked over to the body and toed it. "One to the head, one to the chest."

"I shot the lock, remember?" Fargo said. "Besides, I didn't even know this man, Scotty MacKenzie."

"But earlier he was asking all kinds of questions," the clerk put in, nervously combing his hair with his fingers. "Downstairs, when he checked in. Real curious questions."

"The hell I did!" Fargo shot back. "I just asked who they were. That doesn't prove anything."

"Proves you were interested," the sheriff said mildly, sticking Fargo's Colt into his belt. A couple of deputies appeared in the doorway, guns in hand.

"It proves nothing," Fargo said, exasperated. "Look, Sheriff, you told me yourself this afternoon, a man's not guilty until proven. Can't you see Julie MacKenzie is scared of Sam Blade? She's covering up for something and I'm the fall guy."

"That's a good story, Mr. Fargo," Sikes said. "But the way I see it, I got a murder and two witnesses. Looks pretty clear to me. We'll get you in front of the judge first thing in the morning. Come on, boys."

The two deputies stepped into the room and one pulled out handcuffs. Sam Blade smiled. Julie refused to look up from the floor. For a moment, Fargo considered running. But he knew it would only make things worse. He'd be a hunted man until he could prove himself innocent. He glanced at her. She knew the truth. And somehow, he felt that she wouldn't let an innocent man go to the gallows. He could see that in her face. No. Once out of sight of Sam Blade, she'd do some thinking and when the judge questioned her, she'd come around. The truth would out. Fargo held his hands out in front of him while the handcuffs were put on.

"I'm sure this is going to get cleared up in front of the judge," Fargo said. "Julie MacKenzie knows I'm innocent. And besides, what kind of motive would I have to bust in here and shoot a stranger?"

Sikes gave a short laugh.

"Well, Mr. Fargo, the whole town heard your motive yesterday afternoon," he said. Fargo shook his head, puzzled, trying to imagine what the sheriff was talking about. "Everybody in town heard you when you jumped up and challenged that lady shooter. She said 'What are you doing in town?' and you said 'I'm looking for something to shoot at.'"

Fargo felt stunned. Sheriff Sikes jammed the barrel of his pistol in Fargo's back as they moved toward the door.

"I heard you, Fargo," Sikes said. "And I thought to myself that I'd better keep an eye on you. Well, you found something to shoot at after all. But we got you now. This is a law-abiding town, Mr. Fargo. And we don't welcome your kind."

Fargo's thoughts whirled as he was pushed from the room. He glanced back at Julie. She sat as if paralyzed, refusing to meet his gaze. It all depended on her now.

"Thank you, Sheriff Sikes," Sam Blade called after them. "I always said Hell's Picket was a fine town."

Fargo spent the night pacing the small cell of the jail. For a couple of hours, he thought of escape. They hadn't found the throwing knife strapped to his ankle, but it was of no use. The bars were thick and the double guards were wary. At dawn, they passed a cup of coffee and a roll through the door.

Then six armed men arrived to escort him to the trial. There was no possibility of escape. For the next few hours, Fargo felt as if he was moving through a bad dream. The trial was a joke, a farce. The circuit judge, who clearly had a hangover, sat behind the sheriff's desk. Sam Blade appeared with Julie MacKenzie on his arm and once again, she refused to look at him, answering the questions put to her by Sheriff Sikes and the judge in a quiet voice or with a nod of her head. And Sam Blade had his story down pat, details and all. At the end, Fargo knew he'd lost and when the gavel came down, the judge got to his feet.

"Guilty of the shooting murder of Scotty MacKenzie," the judge said, swaying slightly. He hiccuped. "I charge Mr."—he looked down at the papers on the desk before him—"Mr. Skye Fargo to be hanged by the neck until dead."

There was a muffled cry and Fargo saw Julie MacKenzie start to rise to her feet. Then she went white, stumbled, and slumped down in her chair. She had fainted. Sam Blade put his big arm around her and half-carried her out of the room.

The six men closed in on Fargo and hustled him outside. Justice had not been done after all. Now he would have to find a way of escape so he could prove his innocence another way, outside the law. But escape how? His hands were still cuffed and the six men surrounded him. All armed, all careful. The late morning sun blazed down. He was marched through the dusty streets as the citizens of Hell's Picket pointed at him and muttered to one another.

"Murderer!" one of the women shouted.

"Hangin's too good for a murderer!" a man put in.

With a sense of unreality, Fargo wondered where the six men were taking him. Then with a cold chill, he saw that they were heading straight toward the main square. Surely, they were not taking him directly from the trial to the gallows? But with every step, reality became clearer to him.

The tall wooden platform came into view, surrounded by the false fronts of the old hotel, Sam Blade's gaudy casino, the windowed shops. The sun beat down and he could hear the grains of dust grinding beneath his boots with every step. The man next to him was holding his pistol in his left hand. Fargo realized if he could swing around and grab for the gun with both hands, he could hold them off, run for a horse, make his escape. It was a long shot, but now it was his only shot.

Fargo faked a stumble, brought up both hands and clubbed the man to his left, who went down groaning. He swung right, his cuffed hands before him and caught the second man with a jaw-shattering arc. He kicked out and a third man went down, holding his groin. Fargo clutched at the man's weapon and felt the warm metal of the gun in his grip just as a heavy blow fell across the back of his neck. The stars exploded in the white hot sky and he felt himself going down.

The heat beneath him woke him up. Sweat was trickling down his face and into his ears. A fly buzzed. There was a heavy drumbeat in his head.

The heat rose around him. It was blasting hot. Where the hell was he?

"I'll give you a hundred," a man called out.

"Why, this hayburner's worth more than that!" another voice said.

"Hundred fifty."

"Two hundred."

"Two ten."

"Sold!"

Fargo forced open his eyes. He lay in the noon sunlight, on the gallows platform. The square was filled with people. They were gathered around a black and white pinto, his Ovaro. Another man came to lead the horse away. As he took its bridle, it balked and resisted.

"A good horse whip'll cure that temper," a man shouted. The crowd laughed.

"He's awake!" someone said.

Immediately, the crowd turned toward him and rough hands pulled at him, helping him to his feet. Fargo realized that the noose was already around his neck. The sheriff stood on the platform with his men.

"We had to take this little knife off you, Mr. Fargo," the sheriff said, swinging the throwing knife in front of his eyes. Obviously, they had searched him more carefully while he'd been unconscious. "And we wanted to wait until you woke up, Mr. Fargo," Sheriff Sikes said. "It ain't sporting to hang somebody who's asleep. You got any last word?"

Fargo realized the end of the trail had finally come. He felt the cool breeze against his sweaty face, the warmth of the sun on his shoulders.

Many a time over the years, he'd faced down death and won. But now, death finally got the upper hand. In front of him was his horse, the loyal Ovaro. Now it belonged to somebody else. He caught a flash of yellow on the front porch of the hotel. Sam Blade and Julie MacKenzie stood there, ready to watch his execution. She knew she was sending an innocent man to his death and yet she didn't speak up. Why? What was the power that Sam Blade had over her? Now he'd never know. All that was left for him to do was to die like a man.

"Any last words?" the sheriff said impatiently. Fargo heard the creak of the trapdoor below him. And he knew it was moments before they pulled the lever and then he would drop into space. If he was lucky, his neck would break and the end would be quick.

"Yeah," Fargo said, loudly. His eyes were on t' figure in yellow on the hotel porch. "I'm an innocent man. Sam Blade killed Scotty MacKenzie. You're hanging the wrong man."

In the silence, Fargo waited for her to call out. To tell the truth, but she never spoke. Instead, he saw her twist her head away, not looking toward him.

Sheriff Sikes nodded to one of his men. Fargo heard the rusty creak of the trapdoor mechanism and felt the boards give way beneath him. As if in slow motion, he felt gravity lay its hand on him and pull him downward into space, felt himself dropping down, down, the thick rough rope around his neck, down. There was nothing that could save him now.

WHISPERS OF THE RIVER
BY TOM HRON

They came from an Old West no longer wild and free—lured by tales of a fabulous gold strike in Alaska. They found a land of majestic beauty, but one more brutal than hell. Some found wealth beyond their wildest dreams, but most suffered death and despair. With this rush of brawling, lusting, striving humanity, walked Eli Bonnet, a legendary lawman who dealt out justice with his gun ... and Hannah Twigg, a woman who dared death for love and everything for freedom. A magnificent saga filled with all the pain and glory of the Yukon's golden days....

from **SIGNET**